More Praise for *Loverboys*

"A striking collection of short stories that assemble and break any number of gender and cultural stereotypes. . . . Castillo's particular blend of ingredients is very eclectic and at the same time very American." —*Philadelphia Inquirer*

"These short stories mix idioms, icons, and entertainment styles. . . . Castillo is a funny and delightful performer."
—*Seattle Times*

"Good moments of insight and humor . . . an appealing sense of Bohemia. . . . Castillo is a writer with a great range."
—*Los Angeles Times*

"All of Castillo's narrators tell us their sometimes hilarious, sometimes heartbreaking stories with tenderness and understanding. . . . The language in *Loverboys* is direct and delicious. . . . The prose is at times intimate and conversational. At other times, it is lyrical, philosophical, and eloquently graceful. Ana Castillo is a first-rate storyteller."
—*Bloomsbury Review*

"Castillo achieves a rare melding of power and validity."
—*Boston Globe*

"Castillo's writing is saturated with the vibrant images and pungent smells of the Latino world." —*Newcity Chicago*

"Castillo dramatizes her characters so effectively, readers will keep turning pages. . . . A mixture of revelations and nice surprises. If its goal is to highlight the quirky, painful, and unpredictable nature of love, it succeeds."
—*Washington Post Book World*

Loverboys

S·T·O·R·I·E·S

by Ana Castillo

W. W. NORTON & COMPANY

New York London

The following stories have been previously published: "Subtitles" in *Mirrors Beneath the Earth* (Curkstone Press, 1992). "Being Indian, a Candle Flame, and So Many Dying Stars" in *Prairie Schooner* (Winter 1994) and *Daughters of the Fifth Sun* (Putnam, 1995). "Loverboys" in *Bomb Magazine* (Spring 1993) and *Tasting Life Twice* (Avon Books, 1995). "Conversations With An Absent Lover on a Beachless Afternoon" in *Chicago Stories* (City Stoop Press, 1991). "Ghost Talk" in *Cuento Chicanos: A Short Story Anthology* (University of New Mexico Press, 1984). "Christmas Story of the Golden Cockroach" in *A Gathering of Flowers* (Harper & Row, 1990). "Juan in a Million" in *U.S.A. Weekend*, 1996.

For information about permission to reproduce
selections from this book, write to Permissions,
W. W. Norton & Company, Inc.,
500 Fifth Avenue, New York, NY 10110

For information about special discounts for bulk
purchases, please contact W. W. Norton Special Sales at
specialsales@wwnorton.com or 800-233-4830

Manufacturing by Courier Westford
Book design by Charlotte Staub
Production manager: Devon Zahn

Library of Congress Cataloging-in-Publication Data

Castillo, Ana
Loverboys: stories / by Ana Castillo
p. cm.
ISBN 0-393-03959-5
I. Title
PS3553.A8135L68   1996
813'.54—dc20   95-52048
                                                              CIP

ISBN 978-0-393-33167-7 pbk.

W. W. Norton & Company, Inc.
500 Fifth Avenue, New York, N.Y. 10110
www.wwnorton.com

W. W. Norton & Company Ltd.
Castle House, 75/76 Wells Street, London W1T 3QT

1 2 3 4 5 6 7 8 9 0

*To all the women and the men
who ever loved me
a little bit.*

◁ CONTENTS

◁ LOVERBOYS

Two boys are making out in the booth across from me. I ain't got nothing else to do, so I watch them. I drink the not-so-aged house brandy and I watch two boys make out. It's more like they're in the throes of passion, as they say. And they're not boys, really. I think I've seen them around before, somewhere on campus maybe. Not making out though.

One gets up, to get them each another drink I guess, and he and I check each other out briefly as he passes me up on his way to the bar. He's a white boy wearing a T-shirt with a graphic of Malcolm X on it.

This is the way my life is these days or maybe it's a sign of the nineties: a white boy with a picture of Malcolm X on his T-shirt and me, sitting here in a gay bar trying to forget a man.

Well, okay. He must not have been just any man and I'm sure not just any woman. Before him there were only women. Puras mujeres (¡sino mujeres puras)! A cast of thousands. Women's music festivals, feminist symposiums, women of color retreats and camp-outs, women's healing rituals under a full moon, ceremonies of union and not-so-ceremonious reunions, women-only panels and caucuses at conferences, en fin, women ad infinitum.

And then one day a boy—not much older than either of these two loving it up in front of me, nor the half-dozen other clientele here on a dead Monday night for that matter—comes into my store asking for a copy of *The Rebel*. I point in the direction of Albert—whom once I was so fond of we were on a first-name basis—and he, the boy in my store, kind of casually goes over to check out what we got on the shelf. We're always stocked up on the existentialists, so I didn't bother to offer assistance.

My partner—who used to be my partner in all senses of the word and whom I bought out a year ago—and I opened up the store about ten years ago. We thought about making it a woman's bookstore, a lesbian bookstore, a gay and lesbian bookstore, a "Third World" bookstore, or even an exclusively Latina bookstore. Heaven knows, any town could use at least one of each of those kind of bookshops—stocked up on alternative-press publications that inform you about what's going on with the majority of the population when you sure don't hear it from the mass media. You know? But no, spirituality won out—since all roads eventually lead to one place, we reasoned.

So along with Camus, Sartre, and Kierkegaard, we . . . I carry almost anything you can imagine that comes out of the East and Native imaginations and ancient practices.

I sat back and picked up the book I was reading. I let the boy browse. I saw him leafing through some other things and, finally, he came over with a copy of *The Stranger*.

"Didn't you see *The Rebel* up on the shelf?" I asked, not really looking at him, just taking the book and ringing it up.

"Yeah. But I don't think I'm ready for it," he answered. "I

read this in high school. I think I'll read it again . . . I really like this translation anyway," he said, referring to the edition he had chosen.

I rang it up. But he didn't pick up his package right away. Just kept looking at me. I looked back and smiled, a little cockily. I'm a mirror that way. You look at me a certain way and I respond in kind. Just like with this white guy here who just passed me by again with two Coronas. He looks. He doesn't smile. He just looks like I don't belong here. *I* don't belong here? I helped start this joint about twelve years ago when you couldn't find a gay bar within ten miles of this town.

Me and Rosie and her compadre, who's over there tending bar—the big guy with the Pancho Villa charm and beer belly. He looks like someone's father, right? Not the kind of bartender you would expect to find in a gay bar. Well, just for the record, he *is* somebody's father. His oldest son enlisted in the air force—overcompensating for his dad's dubious machismo or patriotism, if you ask me. He just got shipped off to the Middle East last week. His daughter, Belinda, Rosie's godchild, got married last summer.

That's the way it goes.

Yeah. His wife knows he owns this bar. And she knows all the rest, too. But she's pretty religious and would never have thought to divorce him. Besides, Rosie told me that his wife really doesn't find the men in her husband's life a threat to her marriage. He's got it pretty good, huh?

Anyway, I say to this young man with Indian smooth skin like glazed clay, and the offhanded manner of a chile alegre if I ever saw one, after he's been staring at me for a good minute or so without saying anything, "Is there anything else I can help you with?"

His dark face got darker when he blushed, and he laughed

a little, "Naw, naw . . .," he said, shaking his head. "Actually, I *did* wanna get that one of his, too, but I can't afford it till payday," he admitted, referring to *The Rebel*.

Liking his white, uneven teeth, although I'm not very good with quotes, except to massacre them usually, I said, " 'I was placed halfway between poverty and the sun.' " With that he got this expression like I had just done a wondrous thing by quoting Albert spontaneously. I was ready to part the sea if I could continue to elicit that gaze of a devotee from those obsidian eyes, so I dared to continue quoting: " 'Poverty kept me from thinking all was well under the sun and in history; the sun taught me that history was not everything . . . ' "

He laughed out loud. He laughed like he had just discovered he was in the presence of Camus himself and he slapped his thigh, as if to say, "What a kick!" He stared at me some more and then he left, still laughing.

After that it was all out of our hands. He came back a few more times that week and finally one evening just before I closed. He wasn't buying anything, just browsing and talking with me when I had a minute between customers. By this time we were old chums—talking about all kinds of things, literature mostly. He likes poetry. He writes poetry. Well, at least he says he does. He never showed me anything. But who am I to question or to judge?

So we went to get a taco down the street at my favorite taco joint. I'm really a creature of habit, no doubt about it. There's only one place where I go for tacos and only one place where I go to get loaded. And there's my store. In between is home and sleep.

Anyway, then we came here, as you might have guessed, to have a drink. I used to come just on weekends but since about the time when we stopped hanging out I am here just about every night of the week, it seems.

That night we got pretty "hammered," his favorite word for what we used to do very well together—besides make love. We made love anytime, anyplace, as often as we could—like a happy pair of rabbits—with the one big difference that I don't reproduce—never did when I could and now I never will.

He's really gonna hate me for telling you all this (and I don't doubt that he'll find out someday that I have, since it was the very fact that I'm kind of a public person that scared him off), but little by little, his PMS started to get the better of him. You know, his "Pure Macho Shit." Maybe it's not fair to call what he started to feel towards me that, but I don't know what else it was. I can't explain none of it. I don't know why he's gone, why I'm here worrying about it . . . why *you're* here, for that matter . . .

Except to drink. And we know how far that will get you. It's just like that Mexican joke with the two drunks just barely hanging on to their bar stools. "Well, why do *you* drink?" one asks the other. "I drink to forget," the other guy replies. "And what's it you're trying to forget?" the first guy asks. The other looks up, kind of thinking for a bit, then says, "I dunno. I forgot."

Well, it's a lot funnier in Spanish. Or maybe you have to be Mexican. But for sure, you have to be a drunk to get it . . . or maybe just drunk.

I went over to the pay phone when I first got here and tried to call him. Although I promised myself never to look for him again, I broke down finally—because between books and drinks, there's only him in my head, like one of those melodies where you only know half the words. I called him without thinking about it, like I had done so many times before, and him always on the other end, and pretty soon, he would be with me.

I called the gas station where he *used* to work 'cause I can't call his house, but apparently he's not gigging there anymore. The guy that answered couldn't tell me anything. High turnover in those places is all the consolation he could give me.

Where do you think my boy went? Fired, most likely. Left town, maybe? I doubt it. He's not ready for that kind of wandering, the kind of wandering his soul takes when he's alone and the kind of wandering loving me gave his imagination. Unless I really underestimated him.

Well, see, in the beginning he seemed very cool about my life. The fact that I had not been with a man since college, just women . . . one woman mostly. Considering himself a sensitive progressive politically conscious self-defined young male of color—*of course* he was cool about my life, he said. How could he not be, he insisted.

But that didn't stop him from jumping on top of me the first night we were alone, did it?—when he came over to my place with the excuse to drop off a copy of Neruda's *Veinte poemas de amor y una canción desesperada* that he bought in Mexico where he lived for a semester as an exchange student.

A bright young man, he was. Is. A bright splendid ray in my life. But like Picasso said, "When you come right down to it, all you have is your self. Your self is a sun with a thousand rays in your belly. The rest is nothing." But for a while, he was all mine. Mio. Mio. Mio.

Then his brothers started ragging him about running around with a lesbian—or worse, a bisexual, nothing more shady or untrustworthy (except for a liberal)—who plays soccer and who knows how to do her own tune-ups and oil change. And his mother, about me being a woman with a past. And his father, about me being an independent businesswoman, and what could he teach an older woman?

As if my loverboy were not tormenting himself well enough

on his own day and night over all this as it was. Once he was reading a book by a male psychologist that talked about the history of goddess worship and said that in early times the pig and cow represented the female and were considered powerful deities. So one night we were sleeping and his body gave a great jerk and we both woke up. He told me, "I was dreaming that I was at home in the kitchen and I was telling my brothers that a pig was after me . . . and suddenly this huge pig leaped right through the window at me . . . and I jumped!"

Well, of course it didn't take a genius to figure out who the pig was but I was pretty impressed by his metaphorical interpretation of what I was in his life. He was cool about us for a while, as I said, although he did spend the first months doing some hard drinking over it. Then he sobered up so that he could sort it all out with a clear head, he said.

And then he left.

I went on with my business without missing a beat. You know, I got the store to run. And I spoke at a pro-choice rally last weekend. I started dating a woman I met some time back who had asked me to go out with her before, but I was too busy being in love with an existentialist Catholic pseudo-poet manito fifteen years younger than me to have noticed even Queen Nefertiti herself gliding by on the shoulders of two eunuchs. ¡Jijola! Was I cruisin' for a bruisin'—¿o qué?

I stopped drinking too. You know? For about a week. I couldn't take the hangovers, I told my new friend, who was already frowning pretty seriously on the extent of my alcohol consumption. "You drink too much," she told me at the end of our first date as she walked me to my door. Then she turned around and left me standing there feeling bare-assed with my drunkenness showing and my broken heart, which I would not admit to no matter what. Like everybody, she comes from a dysfunctional family and all that brings up too much stuff for her, she said.

But the funny thing was that when I stopped drinking, I didn't feel any better about him, but I did feel worse about *her*. I just took a good, hard, sober look at her one day and thought, who wants someone around who's gonna be telling you about yourself all the time? Especially when you haven't asked her for her opinion in the first place.

So I told her last Sunday that we were gonna have to be just friends and we talked about it for a while on the phone (I didn't have it in me to tell her to her face) and she said, "Fine, I understand."

Yeah, yeah, yeah. After we hung up I went out. I came here, naturally, and around closing time I made it back home, seeing cross-eyed and hardly able to find the keyhole to get my key in the door when I jumped back and would have screamed like a banshee except that nothing came out of my mouth I was so scared by something moving suddenly out of the darkness coming right at me. And there she was. She had been sitting on the front porch all night waiting for me.

Now, I ask you: Is there justice to this life at all? Or maybe the question should be: Is life even supposed to make sense? Or maybe we shouldn't bother trying to figure it out, just go about our business tripping over it like that crack in the sidewalk that sends you flying in an embarrassing way and when you look back to see what tripped you, and everybody's looking at you, there's nothing there.

I mean, I have been half out of my mind since I said goodbye to my loverboy and I ain't heard nor seen hide nor hair of him since; and meanwhile this woman, whom I forgot the moment I hung up the phone saying goodbye, is convinced that God has put her on this planet for the sole purpose of rescuing me from myself!

Yeah, you heard right just now. I know I said earlier that he left me. But it was me who suggested we not see each other anymore. I mean, it was just a suggestion, right? A damn good one I thought at the time, driven by my self-respect as I am, since he had just told me that he was gonna take a trip and travel around South America with a college friend of his, and didn't know exactly when we'd see each other again. So I decided to give him a head start on feeling what it was to not see me anymore and said I was gonna be pretty busy myself and as of that moment didn't know when *I* could see *him*.

Well, let me tell you how it was with us. We had done all the hokey things people in love do. We stayed up in bed for hours after making love, just talking, confessing all our childhood traumas to each other; we cried together about a lot of things. We went to the zoo, the movies; we took walks and had picnics. We even kissed in the rain, making out in the downpour like nobody's business.

Which of course, it wasn't. He said to me once, "You are the kind of woman who deserves to be kissed in front of everybody."

We had only one fight in all those months. I don't remember what stupid thing started it, but the next thing I know I threw a cushion at him that must've been tearing already because it hardly had an impact and there was fluff all over the place like it was snowing in the room. Well then, he throws a cushion at me. And before you know it, we're laughing and pounding each other with *almohadas destripas*, a flurry of feathers and fluff all over the room.

That's the way it was with us. A lot of laughs. A lot of good times. It's real hard to find someone to laugh with, you know?

Like, you see those two guys still sitting there in the dark? Now they're not smooching anymore. In fact, it looks like they're a little pissed off at each other. Who knows why? I was sitting here since before they came in and never once did those two laugh with each other. They came in, sat down without a word, and as soon as the one got the other a drink, they started making out. Now, they're mad at each other.

But those two will probaby grow old together because they really know how to be mad at each other, while me and my loverboy who didn't have a bad moment together have already gone up in smoke—with the force of burning copal and all the professed tragedy of La Noche Triste—succumbing to our destiny. Between the sun and poverty there was us for a little while.

Well, someone had to take my lunch away. I don't mind admitting it. I hurt Rosie pretty bad after being with her all our adult lives, practically. I just fell out of love with her and even out of like, since we fought so much toward the end. Actually, I know by then that she was seeing that woman who she ran off to Las Cruces with. But she would never admit to that. I couldn't prove it, but I knew it in my heart— the little emaciated excuse for a heart I had left when she took off. But I can't say I blame her for leaving since it wasn't happening with us anymore.

Anyway, I don't really know why I'm telling you about Rosie. That's all over with. But it's like the one who matters is too hard to talk about. I can't talk about it without thinking I look ridiculous—like the classic jilted older woman. Of course it wasn't going to work out. *I* knew that. *He* knew that. And his family didn't help it any either. But even so. Somewhere in the middle of all its fatality, *we*, me, him, even his mother, who was busy having Masses said for her son's salvation—and I'm not putting down his mother either, in case you ever run into him and tell him any of this—*she* knew that what we had was indelible.

I'm gonna stop drinking. This time not because someone

is shaming me out of it. And not because I can stand to go to bed at night thinking of him or waking up alone remembering waking up with him. But because it doesn't help anymore.

I'm gonna stop torturing myself in all the ways that I've been doing; I'll even stop playing all those Agustín Lara records he brought over—for us to make love to. And we did, over and over again.

I saw Agustín Lara perform in Mexico City when I was a kid. Did you know that? He was gaunt and very elegant. My mother was swooning. I was just a little kid, so I was just there. But when I mentioned it to my loverboy, he gave me the sign of la bendición—implying that I was among the blessed to have laid eyes on the late, great, inimitable saint of Mexican music:

Santa, santa mía, mujer que brilla en mi existencia . . . His saint he called me, his saint and his treasure. His first and only love.

I've been thinking about renting the storefront next to my bookstore and extending my business to include a café. You know, café latte, avocado-and-sprout croissant sandwiches, and natural fruit drinks. I think this town is ready for a place like that. Maybe I'll exhibit local artists there, not that there are too many good ones around. But there are a few who are going places—I'll get them to show in my establishment before they do . . .

I think he already split town with his friend; he's probably somewhere in Veracruz at Carnival at this very moment—having a great old time. Well, at least for his sake, I hope so.

You think that maybe he misses me a little bit?

Probably the saddest boy in Mexico right now, you say?

I hope so.

Let me tell el compadre over there to send those two unhappy lovers a couple of beers, on me. There's something insupportable about being pissed with the one person on this planet that sends your adrenaline flowing to remind you that you're alive. It's almost like we're mad because we've been shocked out of our usual comatose state of being by feeling something for someone, for ourselves, for just a moment.

He made me feel alive, cliché or not. Drunk or sober. If he ever finds out I told you all this, he'll really be furious. I guess he felt like he was living in a glass bowl with me. Not that I'm not discreet, but everyone in town seems to know me, or at least think that they do. But I like my privacy, too, you know? Mis cosas son mis cosas. I just had to talk to somebody about it. Been carrying it around inside me like a sin, a crime, like that guy in *Crime and Punishment*. And it wasn't like that at all—far from it.

Anyway, I haven't used any names, in case you didn't notice, not even yours—even though people'll figure it out soon enough. And everybody already knows who I am. I run the only bookstore in town that deals with the question of the soul. All roads sooner or later will lead you there.

◁ WHO WAS
JUANA GALLO?

They even named a drink after her. It's made the same as a margarita, except instead of tequila, you use mezcal. That's because mezcal is the official drink of Zacatecas—her hometown, Zacatecas, Zacatecas, United States of Mexico. Mezcal is also made from the cactus, like the tequila. Very smooth. But of course, it always comes down to a question of taste.

And who was Margarita? I don't know. But I know who Juana Gallo was and if you have the time and with your gracious permission, of course, I will tell you. I am the only one who can. I am the only one left who knew her.

Yes, I know, they made a movie named after her, of course, years ago now. You know what they say, if not for the Revolution of 1910 there would have been no material to build a movie industry on in Mexico. But that movie has nothing to do with Juana Gallo—the real one. Nothing at all. Although María Felix was quite good in the role of an anti-Porfirista soldier. That woman (woman I say, but with nothing but respect—after all, señoras in those days were plenty, while women have always been few), that woman, as I said, always fit the part of the revolutionary very well, a set of ammunition belts strapped across her splendid chest, that famous haughty eyebrow lifted high, and the way she insisted on addressing a man. That is to say, that no matter who he was or who he thought he was before meeting up with her, she'd put any man in his place right then and there. At least in the movies.

I think in real life, too. But who can say? María Felix has outlived all her husbands and all her friends, so I guess there are no witnesses to testify to the contrary.

In the movie of Juana Gallo she loses her man to the dead fly widow played by Dolores del Río. I was never quite convinced of that version of Juana Gallo's life. The captain has Dolores del Río's husband shot. This has happened before the story begins so the viewer never knows the reason for the order, perhaps it was for treason or maybe because the captain didn't like the man's looks. That's the way it was a lot of the time. Juana Gallo's captain was a Zapatista, a revolutionary. It goes to show you, it doesn't matter what side you're on when you're poor. Either way you get shot, if not in the beginning, in the end!

The Mexican army was very abusive about the way it dealt with people, too. Perhaps I'm stepping out of line to say it, but I think some of that still goes on. I hear tell over in the state of Guerrero there has been trouble lately and of course in Chiapas, for a long time. Little has changed in this whole century. But who am I to say? No one and nobody. Just a poor so and so who can't keep his mouth shut when he's supposed to, that's what they tell me.

Who are these "they" to whom I keep referring? Well, come to think of it, I can't quite honestly say. I've always wondered the same thing myself. But they do appear to have a lot to say about how one runs his life, wouldn't you agree?

In any case, it seems to me, at least from the movie version of the story, that it was a combination of pity and his hypocritical virtue that the captain chose the pious weeping widow over a woman like Juana Gallo as played by la doña. Juana Gallo/ María Felix was the kind of woman who would kill for her man. And did, I think, a few times. Dolores del Río as the widow, if I am remembering correctly, actually took the captain's alms which he handed to her in order to relieve his conscience. Imagine—accepting his pity!

Now Juana Gallo/María Felix, she was the kind of woman who would take off all her clothes in plain day to make love. Dolores as widow cloaked from head to toe in black in the sweltering sun probably didn't even make a little noise when a man slipped his callused hands under her long skirts. Although I must admit at once that while it may have more to do with my years in the seminary than with anything else, there *is* something erotic in the scene where the captain on horseback catches a glimpse of the widow bathing in the river fully clothed and when she realizes she is being watched, she flushes with embarrassment.

"Well, I would be embarrassed too, if anyone found out that I bathed with all my clothes on!" la doña might say to that.

In any case, that movie, as entertaining as it may be, wasn't based on facts. Although some people around town do believe it, it's because they didn't know her. As for the widow played by Dolores del Río, she was pure invention, a way for the film tycoons in Mexico City to make more money featuring our two biggest stars who were said to be off-screen rivals.

And can you believe it? The two women were actually forced to get into a catfight on-screen.

The way I look at it, there was no contest if one measures it in terms of integrity: One went to Hollywood, the other refused. One accepted supporting roles, the other played second to none. One consented to speaking English, the other raised her eyebrow and went off to Italy, Buenos Aires, France and played the leading lady that she remains to this day.

But forgive my digression and let me tell you about Juana Gallo, as I promised. They say her galán, her cavalier so to speak, was based in the barracks which had been set up in the center of town. This local version also has it that after their breakup she became very pious. Her claim to fame was that she slapped the governor in front of the whole town for his opposition to the church. But how was a woman, the real Juana Gallo, who had a lover (and so openly!) and who was clearly a rifle-toting soldier herself, to be so much on the side of the church?

Of the Ten Commandments, I think that the most popular stories about her conduct had Juana Gallo breaking at least eight, not to mention defying simple logic. How can she be a revolutionary and be devoted to a government officer? But you know, that's not uncommon either, senseless rumors among most people. I'm not saying that Juana Gallo was a hypocrite. I never knew a woman, anyone, man or woman, more driven by her convictions.

Now her captain, *he* was a hypocrite. In real life, the captain she loved and lost was in Portfirio Díaz's army. He did not marry her because, it was said, he had a wife in Jeréz. And there was talk of a second one in Torreón where Villa's troops were based. Jeréz is right next door to Zacatecas so he probably couldn't have gotten away with marrying two women in neighboring towns if he had gotten together with Juana Gallo in that way. Of course, on the other hand, the government was really hard on the church and the captain probably could have married as many times as it occurred to him without worrying about the law or the church giving him a hard time.

The truth of all that part of the story is that Juana Gallo was not the marrying type.

Women can be faithful, the trouble is finding a man to be

faithful to—that is what la Marlene Dietrich said or something like that. Juana Gallo, like the star Maria Felix, and I
suppose like la Marlene Dietrich, too, was of fierce character,
impenetrable as the infinity of stones that comprise her native
land and as loyal to the republic as the city of her birth.

What a fool is all that I can say. What a fool that captain
was to let a woman like Juana Gallo go. A woman who would
kill for her man as I've said, and who did, more than once.

He had been up all night drinking, the famous cavalier,
raising hell with his men, some of his favorites and a few of
the bootlickers. They had a few old cantina women around
too. Juana Gallo didn't care anything about that. She never
had anything to be jealous of, she said, and never was. She
slept peacefully that night.

So, the next morning, when the prisoner—one more poor
goat accused of treason in a war made up of traitors—was
brought before the captain, he really wasn't up to dealing with
the matter properly and as effectively as his post demanded.
So Juana Gallo took the matter into her own deft hands. Even
the bootlickers hadn't been up to shooting the man in cold
blood—his offenses were rather vague to begin with—on a
Sunday morning, just like that. During the revolution, both
sides usually respected Sundays as the day of our Lord. The
bells of the cathedral were pealing loudly and meanwhile,
Juana Gallo, without much formality, said, "Oh. So this bald
one has offended you, my love?" And before the captain could
respond, she pulled the captain's gun right out of his holster
so fast he barely took note of it before the shot went off and
struck the poor cabrón—pardon that I put it so crudely but
that's how it was—right between the eyes, a word of denial
suspended in his mouth.

Two of the captain's favorites bent over heaving, saying it
was all the mezcal from the night before and not the brains

and blood that splattered on their cowardly mugs as they watched a woman defend their captain's honor.

Not me. I just stood there without so much as a wince. Nothing has ever moved me. Except Juana Gallo, naturally. They've always said that I don't feel anything because of my Indian blood. That is, that I'm a burro, a mere beast of burden that has only one function in this life and that is to serve. These "they" who always have something to say have a lot of misconstrued ideas, in my opinion. My Indian blood must be as strong as a burro's whipped raw hide for me to have endured as much as I have as long as I have, but it has nothing to do with my heart. It's all in there. It's as heavy as a full bladder, too, una bufa. That's the Basque word for it, *bufa*. Everyone around here knows that word. They were the ones who conquered these lands and they named that peak over there la bufa. We used to call all the hills and all the mountains "Mother." The conquistadores named our highest peak "bladder."

Before King Felipe II baptized this land the City of Our Lady of Zacatecas and confirmed it with the title the Very Noble and Loyal City, it was the land of the Tecuexes, Huachiles, and the Caxcanes—various Chichimec tribes—and of course, los Zacacatecos, the grass people, my ancestors.

Juana Gallo was a mestiza of course, you know, of mixed blood. But unlike most of the people around here she didn't deny her Indian blood. And she did not look down on those of us who cannot deny it even if we wished.

As for the rumors of her piety, she was Mexican, no reason to say more! Of course she was Catholic. She attended evening Mass, at least for a time during her long life, but not ever regularly. When she did she gave whatever she had on her when the collection plate was passed. But she was not, thank God, one of those petit bourgeois types so in abundance around here, arm in arm, like stale caramel drops stuck together, making their pilgrimages in clickity-clacking heels and little veils on their dyed heads and all their jewelry flashing in the setting sun, believing that they have put another down payment on their plot in heaven with each novena that they dedicate to Our Lady of Patroncinio.

If you ask me, although no one ever has, they were the very ones who made up the weak link in the revolution, the petit bourgeois. Well, actually, it was their men that were the weak link. The women—they only cared about maintaining their petty comforts (that's why they're called the petit bourgeois), their afternoon chocolate and cakes and canasta parties, their dresses pressed by an eleven-year-old indita who comes to work for them for life in exchange for leftovers and a little floor space to sleep on. They care about their spoiled sons and marrying off their useless daughters well. Nothing more.

No, Juana Gallo was not one of those. She never had children. The vicious tongues around here say she got pregnant but *aborted* each time. They whisper *aborted*, if they utter the word at all, afraid that to say it will earn them a side trip to purgatory. Has anyone told them yet that the church has abolished purgatory? It's really confusing, even to me, who was never convinced about purgatory to begin with. Where did all those souls go when the church decided on that?

I think that when she was very young, even before the cavalier, Juana Gallo would have wanted to be a mother. she loved children very much in the beginning of her life. Her mother sent her to school with the nuns because—I suspect— she hoped that the nuns would keep her. They (this time meaning specifically the nuns) said she had a talent for working with children and recommended that she become a school-teacher. But her parents didn't think formal education should be wasted on a girl. They were simple people. What did they know?

When she grew very old and was dirty always because of the distraction that came with age and poverty, she grew to hate children. They followed her down the street and taunted her all the time. That is when nobody really remembered anything about her, not even her real name, since Juana Gallo is not her Christian name, of course. She carried a big stick this size and would try to swat them. And the children would just laugh and taunt her even more because of course she always missed.

I asked the young girl who runs the tobacco shop right in front of the last house where Juana Gallo lived, "Do you know where Juana Gallo's house can be found?" She didn't have a clue. She didn't even know who Juana Gallo was. She thought I was asking about anybody, someone who is still around. She just looked ahead, into the air, at who knows what, and said only, "No." And here we were, both standing right in front of it, a point of historical interest. For anyone but her, I suppose. She, with her handmade broom sweeping the steps, and me, just testing the youth, as always.

From the looks of it, this country won't have any hope at all come next century. It's a wonder we've come this far.

The other version you hear of Juana Gallo around here is that she was a heartless soldadera, a soldier on the side of the rebels, bringing soldiers down with the best of the Zapatistas. There's no connection with her and the army or any cavalier for a lover. This version includes the ugly one of her final days as an old senile wench, but it is said, in a whisper again, because sins cannot be pronounced without causing some taint to the soul I suppose, that as a young woman she was a lesbian.

I suppose that to make her a lesbian implies that women had to watch out for her, run from her, as they had to do with the soldiers—on both sides of the battle. Moreover, to act like

Juana Gallo in any way was to act like a man. But as far as I ever noticed anything regarding that suspicion, although she herself had no use for gossiping biddies during embroidery sessions, she got along well with women, the market vendors and with all the housewives. Mostly, she kept to herself all her life.

It's true that she never married. But what does that mean anyway?

The truth is that Juana Gallo was a woman, plain and simple, and a plain and simple woman. She didn't put on airs and she dressed like any woman you might see walking down the street on her way to buy the day's provisions. In her time, because I remember it all very well, she was quite lovely to look at: smooth, smooth skin, big, big eyes, and a smile to enchant whomever. What else is there to say?

During that epoch, that is, during the days of the revolution, most of the humble people, from which she also descended, were pro-agrarian reform. But we could not say it aloud. We went about our business, heads bowed when we passed the barracks in the center of town, so as not to get stopped and shot, just for making eye contact

And yes, it is true, she did pick up a rifle for a time and traveled with the revolutionaries. When Juana Gallo came back she had earned the name Juana Gallo.

She did, I believe, slap the governor in front of the whole town, but that would have been because he deserved it, not in defense of any institution. And only she would have had the nerve to put him in his place. Maybe because she was a woman he did not have her imprisoned for life or worse, not then and there, not ever. Or maybe because she was Juana Gallo.

The only thing I know for a fact is the following: I loved Juana Gallo. Yes, I loved her with all my heart.

◁ If Not for the Blessing of a Son

So it came to pass that after nearly twelve years of marriage God blessed them with a child. They were blessed twofold with a boy child. And blessed that much more since the couple were both past their youth and the chances of having another child again in their lives seemed unlikely.

It was about that time that a coup d'état befell the country and as the new father had once held the position of minister of something or other, having been close friends with the deposed president since their soccer days in college, the couple decided it was wisest to flee and with their newborn began a new life in Florida in the United States of America.

The father did not ever obtain a post in his newly adopted country having anywhere near the prestige and recognition of minister of something in the government, but he was fortunate in landing a secure teaching position in a local university and the couple led a satisfying life with regards to their comforts and lifestyle.

By the time the boy reached the age of entering kindergarten, the father had successfully established himself as a pillar of his community. The mother, also, as a good wife, mother, and Catholic woman, was said to be every bit the perfect match for her fine husband.

They bought a home. They drove a new car. But they did not, however, ever flaunt their financial success, which would have been insensitive and undermining to those others in their community, which consisted of a wide variety of immigrants from their homeland, many whom had not had the couple's same luck or sense of perseverance.

Many times the father would say to his wife at the dinner table, "Only you know, querida, what I had to do in order to get established in this country." And she would nod, and pick up the platter of fried bananas or rice and add an unsolicited spoonful to his place in a gesture that he interpreted subconsciously as his reward for all he had had to do to get established in the United States. It was a fair interpretation since his wife had unconsciously added the spoonful of rice or fried bananas because it was her only way of expressing her gratitude for all he had done and buy all the same kinds of lovely things they had enjoyed in their homeland, not to mention secure her position with the women in their community as someone they should unquestionably respect and in some cases, envy.

The boy was very beautiful physically, having taken after neither father nor mother but his paternal grandmother, who had been, family legend had it, a Spanish gypsy. This was never confirmed because his grandmother died giving birth to his father and the grandfather had sent his only son away to school and never had established the kind of familial relationship in which such a question might be asked, let alone answered.

He had been given the names of both grandfathers, a decision equally satisfying both parents and leaving both quite satisfied that as a Christian couple they had done their duty to both family and God by bringing forth this boy child and giving him a legacy of paternal family names.

Before he started school he had spent his days in the sole care of his mother. While his father did not question her maternal abilities, he did however express occasional concern that, having no other children to share her affection with and given her age, she might be overprotective and therefore orient their son to be fearful of life.

This made the mother sensitive to the doting she might have given her only child and so she quite consciously held her affections for him in reserve. She did this in particular in the presence of the father.

But it would have been all fine, if this were all there was to this story which is nothing if not a common one of how boys are made into men. And it was known that this couple had done that precisely, with the refinement of generations of practice, when after college graduation their son, who still lived with them in that one and only home he had ever known in Florida, decided his calling was to join the police department.

At first his parents expressed to both their only son as well as their now old friends and compadres their disappointment in such a common and vulgar career choice.

It became particularly disturbing for the mother, poor thing, who already envisioned losing her only child in the line of duty given the hideous crime rate in the city, when one of her compadres, who was having dinner with them that evening, asked exactly why it was that he, the son, so desired to be a law official and the son smiled broadly and said offhandedly, "I want a license to kill . . ."

The compadre stared without comment, fork in hand in midair, and the mother, so upset, jumped out of her chair and went to the kitchen pretending to have forgotten something on the table. But the father did not hide his objection and slammed his fist on the table. Red-faced he turned to his son, as he so often had done as the boy grew up into a man, disregarding the presence of others, and pointed his finger in his son's nose, "*You* . . . are an ungrateful hijo de la mierda!"

His son broke out in a sweat as he often did when his father yelled at him. He pushed back his wire-rimmed glasses that slipped down his nose and lowered his head.

After scenes such as this, it was common for the mother to expect her son to come down with something. It was usually a fever, sometimes worse. Since he started school at the age of five she had resigned herself to the fact that her son was indeed physically and perhaps emotionally delicate. Since childhood he had had recurring strep throat and "pinkeye." Having the flu each winter was not uncommon for him. By the age of twelve he had undergone several operations for some not-life-threatening maladies, including tonsillitis, appendicitis, as well as one which was quite serious and had to do with his irises and which resulted in his permanent need for glasses. He had grown tall and apparently strong. He ran up to ten miles every morning before sunrise. He alone had felled that nuisance of a tree in the backyard that his father had refused to pay to have done once it was obvious that the tree was rotting and couldn't be saved.

In so many other ways, her son had been her light and breath. It was he who helped her with household chores, something that the father could not even jokingly have ever been asked to do. It was her son who could be counted on to run errands, to wash and hand-wax her car every Saturday, cancel appointments on the telephone, write letters for her, load and unload the dishwasher twice a day, walk the dog three times a day, and give her the great pleasure of a twice-weekly pedicure which he had become an expert at since she first taught him when he was six years old.

No, there was no doubt that she could not bear life without her son.

As for the father, he too depended heavily on his son. His son had proven himself adept at financial matters and it was he who had handled all of his father's investments. It was the son again who mowed the lawn and trimmed the hedges as he had been taught to do as a boy. The son took his father's shirts and suits to the cleaners and polished his father's wingtips. He also washed and waxed his father's car, kept his father's home office neat, papers filed, and books in order on the shelves.

In these and many other indispensable ways the son reciprocated for his room and board and education, in addition to the fact that as a good Catholic son it would have been his duty nonetheless. He was not only an only son and only child, his parents were evidently getting on in their years and reminded him of that obvious fact on a daily basis. The son had never held a job outside the home, having had almost no time for it between his studies and the obligations that were not seen as obligations really as much as simply his life.

Consequently, to the world, to all those who came and went out of their home over the years, attended dinners on holidays and Sundays and sat at the table of the most gracious host and hostess of their community and parish, it appeared that the son had grown to be a model individual. What a husband he would be to a young woman someday! He had only to select a woman half the one they saw in his mother to continue the irreproachable standard for family values that his father had set. It had taken him a little longer than most to finish his studies, so it appeared therefore that it would take him a little longer to find a wife worthy of his qualities, as well.

But even the most naive and ingenuous of their often-invited guests—only on Sundays and holidays—might have, should have, perhaps, as the years passed, concluded that only God Himself and men who were far from holy have made themselves irreproachable among men, placed themselves high and apart from all others and have permitted no one to make them accountable for their acts.

But what acts could friends of the family ever have questioned to make their compadre accountable for? Somewhat strict and old-fashioned, perhaps, but that was nothing to criticize. Many of them would have wished they had been able to instill such respect from their own children.

It was also true the father upheld certain anachronistic customs that they themselves had repudiated with their own fathers, such as the one of kissing the father's hand as a greeting. But the son seemed comfortable enough to do it, did so, at least, without hesitation or question, and even did so with certain filial devotion that made observers yearn for long-forgotten patriarchal days in their homeland.

And when outsiders were not around to observe the many other ways the son had been taught to express his affection, the parents, both mother and father, did not hesitate to request it. And not always in the presence or with the knowledge of the other.

So it was that the house on the corner with the creeping trumpet vines, with their orange flowers that the boy once picked and sucked their secret nectars from, robbing both bees and hummingbirds of their right and joy, the immaculately trimmed hedges and finely cut green lawn, the polished cars parked side by side in the driveway and the dog that never barked in its little house in the backyard, had become, and remained for the son, the house of secrets.

◁A PERFECT ROMANCE

He was a newborn angel and she, a glorious (if not disorienting) sight for him, seated on a golden throne, with a dark, child-size hand beckoning him forth.

This was one dream, which he nevertheless had with his eyes open.

Another was to sniff her panties. (A woman with silk panties and yet who complained about the cost of bread, who in fact went without bread in order to afford the panties.)

A third dream was unspeakable, even to himself. All that he might have said of it was that in the end, she was a void.

She, too, had dreams of him and never with her eyes closed. She said: "I see you with me at the John F. Kennedy airport. We have our passports," or "We are in a couchette and you are getting up to get me a bottle of Evian," or "We are standing in front of the Museum of Science and Industry in Chicago. It is the end of winter and still a little cold."

Her dreams were very specific, while his were filled much more with sensory details.

Another thing that they both had in common aside from

these flights of fantasy, or more precisely, their tendency toward melancholia and escapism, was their delicate constitutions. On more than one occasion she had felt herself light-headed and next found herself facedown on the patio or in the bathroom. He suffered from bouts of nausea.

On their well days, they enjoyed each other's company very much. On one occasion they took a walk in the rain. Neither caught a cold. One Saturday evening they took in a movie. Neither he nor she was a food person, so they rarely ate together.

One afternoon, they were sitting in silence in a small park. Then she said, "You wanted to marry me in the beginning, but you don't now."

"Yes, but I realized that that was right after my divorce and I was acting on impulse."

"You were lying to me then?"

"I suppose I was. But I am not lying to you now."

After a while, they both got up and decided to have a cup of coffee at the cafe at the edge of the park.

At the cafe, she asked, "Do you love me?"

She wondered about her own question. If he said yes, she would still be left to doubt him because of the need she felt to ask the question in the first place. Love, after all, would seem to be a state of being that was obvious, self-revelatory, not stated, not made actual by the saying of it. If he said no, she also would not be convinced because by then she thought of him not so much as a liar but as a man who did not know the truth, truth itself being turned into a word at that moment in her mind instead of a state of being, self-revelatory, and she not knowing what it all meant.

"Yes," he said.

"I love you too," she responded, with something of a smile,

and reached over and gently squeezed his hand that was still holding the spoon he had used to stir his coffee.

They walked all the way back to her apartment building. It was getting to be that time when as the sun went down the temperature made a radical drop. "I'm not feeling very well," she said.

"You'd better get some rest," he told her. She returned his jacket which he had taken off and put over her shoulders over the one she was wearing. They parted at the bottom of the stairs.

Later, after she had a light dinner of plain macaronis and red wine, she dreamt of them together on a bus to Juárez. It occurred to her that her dreams of them together were all transient.

For his part, he went home and thought of how black her hair was, as were her eyebrows. "Such black eyebrows," he said to himself aloud, remembering them.

She opened the door to the balcony before going to bed, where she would read until sleep came. It was cool outside but the heat of the day had stayed in the apartment. She saw six cicadas stuck to the screen door. They were very large, larger than grasshoppers. That's how she knew that they were cicadas and not grasshoppers. She wore nothing to bed but picked up the string of pearls tossed on the nightstand and put them on. He liked her pearls.

He wore pajamas. It was the thing to do with others around, after all, since he did not live alone. He went to the yard in his pajamas and tossed a stick for the dog for a bit and then went to bed.

It was quite possible that she would be the love of his life, or was already that. She had asked him that many times. The love of a person's life meant to him that each day the beloved was the source of why one did not feel alone as well as the cause for sensations that overcame one quite unexpectedly, at inconvenient moments sometimes, such as when counting out the day's receipts or when advising a customer on a new product.

She would ask, "Am I the love of your life?" And he would respond, "What do *you* think?"

She would not say what she thought. After all, she had asked a question to get an answer and until she had some kind of answer there was really little material to think from. But because he answered rather whimsically, she never asked twice at one time, but smiled, and would kiss him on the cheek or on the mouth with closed lips.

What they enjoyed best together was ballroom dancing. On three occasions they went to the Holiday Inn downtown and did just that. He was very impressive in his best suit and she, who wore high heels only on those occasions, had perfectly formed calves.

This was probably the only thing perfect about her. But anything that might be considered perfect, even for a moment, or, if only at a particular angle, or, in a certain light, by any measure, deserved reflection.

He thought—he was sometimes certain—that he would think about her all his life.

By ten o' clock, she was always asleep, surrounded by pillows and concluding that if she never were to wake, even once, with him, with him, he had not existed at all.

◁ GHOST TALK

This is the city where it all happened/happens. The one movie directors love so much because the streets make for great chase scenes, cops in hot pursuit of the bad guys; the audience, full of popcorn and candied almonds, turns nauseated as the car rises up and makes a daring leap. Here is the street. i sense the approach to the little Cuban diner with the guanabana juice drinks in cans and those wicked sandwiches on toasted French bread, stuffed with ham and steak. There's the paleteria, right around the corner, next to the santeria shop. You can suck on your coconut popsicle while you decide which potion will be best suited to capture your lover's undying devotion, or drive away the competition.

i catch a glimpse of her profile in a store window. Her hair is cut shoulder length, the Indian braid buried somewhere in a bureau drawer. It is the cut of a woman well on her way to conservative middle age, some days it is lustrous and sexy. You have sexy hair, the hair stylist says, running a comb lovingly through it, then corrects herself as if women are not supposed to say such things to women. My mother said i looked like Greta Garbo and Juana said i should be in an Italian movie. Biased opinions.

Today i look like a ghost of Xmas past. i lived here before, with the braid and faded denims. All the walls are painted with ghosts, vestiges of the great movement, the onset of revolution, the uprising of the people.

i like the cafe, which must be a recent addition to the neighborhood. Great coffees of the world. You can sit in there alone and immerse yourself in a book, sip on an expensive cup of coffee for hours and no one will bother you. It's just you and your latest idol between the pages of the only book that matters in the world. The sun is super bright but it's brisk, ocean cool, and a slight shiver runs over your bare arms when you think of it.

Iraida remembers Habana. It was a small Paris, she tells me. There were people out at all hours of the day or night, and everyone was alive. She plays Afro-Cuban rhythms and educates me on the great cultural contributions Cubans have made to the world. She pecks her temple with a forefinger; we are intelligent people, she says. My father's idol is Pérez Prado, i tell her. She nods. Pérez Prado made his name in Mexico. The operetta. The record scratches some. The daughter of a slave woman and her white master falls in love with his son, her half-brother. She bears a child from him. He marries a white woman of the aristocracy and as the newly wedded couple leave the church, a black man, who is in love with the mulatta, stabs her lover. She finds refuge in the same convent where her mother had gone eighteen years before to give birth to her. Her mother and she pray to the Virgin for forgiveness.

Iraida believes black people deserve everything white people have, but she hasn't been able to shake off her personal prejudice. They still repulse her with their kinky hair and odd features.

i dab a little oil behind the ears to ward off the evils of envy. Envy is the root of all evil, not money, like white people say. My mother-in-law warns me against inciting envy. Don't tell anyone what you have and if they find out, say, it is God's blessing and you're humbly grateful.

i wonder if any of the artists are still around? The ones who published 1,000 copies of their poetry anthologies and ran off 500 silk-screen posters of the latest cause they joined. They may be teaching at Berkeley now, Stanford, or the University of Texas. Maybe they have lucrative jobs at major publishing houses or are still hiding in the same Victorian apartments with tall, bare windows and long corridors crowded with books, record albums, and other cultural paraphernalia, planning and waiting out all the present dictators. It won't be long, they say, sip espresso from cracked, stoneware cups, munch on pieces of stale toast.

Oh! Or maybe they are rolling up those delicious corn tortillas, wickedly fattening, smearing on avocado (it's not called guacamole if it's just avocado) and afterward rolling away like a bloody fat chinche, a bedbug.

You nap, and when you awake, all the neon lights in Chinatown are blinking like a galaxy of stars. It's like NY. You find a little greasy-spoon place and ask the waiter for one thing but he doesn't speak a word of English so you're oh so happy with whatever he brings you, all strange and tasting of the stuff that grows at the bottom of the sea.

Loud blaring radios from low riders and hot young men hoping to get lucky tonight.

You are a ghost, like you were a ghost before because you were never here, but everywhere at once, *i wish i could talk like my eyes can see*, word you with what i smell, knock your socks off with aromas of a tiny metropolis tourists only catch glimpses of at the Wharf. A thousand LSD trips and middle-aged folks remembering Timothy Leary playing like the Pied Piper leading them all off to jump off the pier.

Somebody sewed up my mouth with Indian sealer thread. We are but we don't speak. We listen but we don't hear it, the thunder of buffalo hooves 'cross the plains. i hold my head up high. If i'm a drunkard, i don't know it. i like it, the way it burns swishing down my gut and widens a hole in my liver. The way it makes me smile and remember and forget when i don't want to remember and before i know it i'm talking and telling what maybe i should watch whom i'm telling it to but for the moment, who cares? Someone's smiling back and nodding, pretending to respect it. i'm my age and i ain't been around for nothing, but i ain't seen nothing and i ain't done nothing 'cause no matter how long a being lives, it's not long enough. But i'm glad i made it far enough to come back here.

i remember someone who used to live up that street, and a woman who painted murals who lived in a storefront with enough stuff to start her own museum. A museum of junk. She was all full of herself too, because she was a star in her own right. Now, who can remember her name? i don't. i do remember her contribution. And i'm thankful.

i'm not envious. Like my mother-in-law says, envy is evil. It eats up at you, like maggots, knocks out your eyes from the inside, nibbles away at your tongue and before you know it, no one wants to hear what you have to say because it's all worth that much: food for maggots. Listen: i went from looking like a Campesina to slick clothes, Panama hats and Italian shoes, to just being me again, a Campesina in disguise. i don't want anyone's envy. They can keep it.

i just want respect. That you earn. You put as much effort

into it as making money, but kind of by doing all the complete opposite.

We are sitting in Iraida's kitchen. The old grandmother from upstairs knocks on the door for the third time that day. Did Iraida hear from her son yet? He left the day before and hasn't been heard from. Like a mother, I know what it is to worry about a child, she says. Iraida smiles. He just called. Gave no explanation but it didn't matter. He was alright. Iraida pours the old woman espresso in a tiny cup. You look Cuban, the old woman says. Iraida beams proudly. You look Cuban. Didn't I tell you? Where do you get looking Indian from? The old lady scrutinizes, but she does have a little of that Aztec look about her . . . After she gets past the questions regarding my marital status and i've pulled out a foto of my husband and me, the two women raising eyebrows and commenting on what a big, fine man he is to look at, she asks if i haven't had a family because i didn't want to or couldn't. Couldn't, i say, but my expression looks as if someone has just asked if i take one or two lumps of sugar in my coffee, and i smile politely, none for me, thanks. But as soon as i've let on that i would have a family if i could, both women raise their arms high in the air. Oh no! Each one talks simultaneously. Why do i want to ruin my life with children? All they do is make you suffer! You give your life to raising them for nothing! I've already lost one, says the old woman, he was all grown already too. He was still in Cuba and got sick. He died from a penicillin shot. The last time I saw him, my son was a cadaver.

One of Iraida's sons is manic-depressive.

This is all happening in memory, you see, back home, the windy city, Chi-town, where Latin people with open minds can congregate and share and talk as if we were all just passing through this country. Like it isn't so much a country as a large stretch of territory where one can work and survive and possibly do well enough to go back home to the real country, where palm trees sway the way they don't in Hollywood, and fish tastes like heaven smothered in sautéed onions, garlic, lime, and a variety of peppers. A country belongs to one exclusively. It is synonymous with home. One says, i am going back to "my" country. Bigoted North Americans who forget where their grandparents came from say, Why don't you go back to *your* country. I'd be very happy to, thank you, but *your* people have occupied it.

Anyway, one day Iraida and i work ourselves into a depression. She has placed two bottles of cheap wine before me and i have steadily drunk glass after glass until they are both gone and we have run the gamut on cultural topics from Russian literature to the recent mayoral primary race. We talk about friendship and we nod with wistful smiles. It is beautiful to capture the soul of another being, isn't it? i nod and add, particularly when it has been a special person. We are talking about friendship, that has its own tenets so we are not talking about romantic/love/sex capture of another soul but the true captivation of another's spirit, which happens between people of the same sex sometimes. We are both remembering such an experience, but she tells me that it is magic when it happens and magic cannot be contrived, so perhaps if one gives up that friendship, takes it for granted, does something typically egocentric to jeopardize it, the magic vanishes.

We were snuggled last night watching the late, late movie, a western with Clint Eastwood. Clint has made an art of squinting. It hasn't been a bad winter but it was nippy since we keep the heat down. The gas rates going up 25 percent in one jump and all. The cat snuck under the covers. He falls asleep just before the movie finishes and i can't stand not to know what happens in the end of anything, no matter how uninterested and bored i may have been until then, i just have to know. Did he give up being the roughest, baddest sheriff in the whole territory to settle down with the blond who ran the dry goods store or did he turn his badge in and ride off into the sunset, having been an incurable roamer from the start? i have to tell him how it ended in the morning as we heat up leftovers and squeeze oranges for breakfast. i make up a lie and say Clint was ambushed and shot up like Swiss cheese.

It's not how much you know but what you know, right? So i've read *Crime and Punishment*, am familiar with Beethoven's Fifth (who isn't?), and know that Nietzsche had some concerns about God's lack of tangibility in the human heart. So you put yourself in neutral and cruise all the way through what seems superficially like a very deep discussion.

i don't have a square back like Indians do, and my legs are curved, not birdlike. But i think people don't get past that. They focus on the narrow eyes, dark skin, the full lips and black straight hair. i don't tell anybody my father was white.

He was a foreman of the assembly line where my mother worked when she first came up North. He took her out to eat sometimes. A man twice her age, he already had grandchildren. When my mother got pregnant, he didn't have to fire her. She quit.

She told me he came to see her once after i was born. He gave me a chain with little pearls and a gold heart-shaped locket. i keep it in a tin box on the dresser. My husband's father sent him a photograph of himself on his first birthday. Jerk, he says, whenever his mother pulls it out.

My mother doesn't speak English, i tell everyone. No one believes it after thirty years. So one Saturday we are out shopping. There is a sale on potatoes at one market and another on chicken clear across town. Suddenly my mother is a bronzed statue. Her heavy-lidded eyes close to slivers and i turn to see what has immobilized her. He is very tall, although age has bent his body some and he walks slowly. A much younger woman, about my age, carrying a small child, chatters next to him. She is blond and the child is blond. He is bald so i can't tell what color his hair was. i begin to fantasize. Excuse me, sir, but i have reason to believe i am your daughter. He trembles a bit, looks at me as if i were a ghost, which i am; and the woman next to him gapes like a bird that's being strangled. i believe you owe my mother twenty-one years of child support. Make it out to her and her husband,minus four years, the first year after i was born and the three when i left home. My mother has a fryer in each hand, bits of melting ice drip on the floor. Are you sure, i ask her, and the way she ignores my question has answered it. i wait until the man and his granddaughter and great-grandchild are past the checkout counter and watch to see what car they get into in the parking lot. i memorize the license plate number.

So i'd had enough, the way young people always have had enough, impatient and too wise for their own good, so i left after high school. My husband and i went off to the city where it all happened/happens to become part of it.

For a time we are back there, though. He has a job and i'm feeling good about myself. We think maybe this is the place where we'll stay, until i see the man who was not so much my father as the jerk who pressured a young Mexican woman who didn't speak two words of English, rented a room in somebody's flat and couldn't, would never go home alone with a child, and then went on with his life, to his little bungalow in the white/Polish/Lithuanian part of town, with their immaculate front yards and one-car garages.

It was just like i pictured it. His wife had probably passed away by then, no vegetable garden or rose bushes in the back anymore. He was most likely retired, spent his days watching

TV and baby-sitting. His station wagon was in the driveway. i rang the bell three times, then went around back and knocked on the kitchen door. When i came around front, he was at the door, looking around. He had that fear of old people who worry about strangers knocking on their doors. And when our eyes met he showed another kind of fear. Mexicans might be moving into the neighborhood.

But i showed him all my official papers and assured him that City Hall was an equal opportunity employer. i was working for the mayor's new department on the concerns of senior citizens. i only needed a few minutes of his time to ask a few questions.

He never smiled, but when i sat on the reupholstered couch across from his favorite chair, crossed my legs so that the skirt slipped up above the knee, i saw how his eyes licked my skin and i aroused an old familiar yearning. We were done in a few minutes, as i told him. When i put my important papers back into the attaché case, he got up and asked if i didn't want a cup of instant coffee or a Nehi orange drink, the kind that's always on sale. i said, fine, thank you, whatever's not too much trouble.

When he came back from the kitchen with a glass of orange soda with ice, i had the gun out and casually brought it up with an agile left hand pointing it at him. Sit down, Old Man, i said and smiled. He dropped the glass. Orange soda soaked into the gold carpeting. He looked around. Maybe he was waiting for one of his grandchildren, or hoped one might pop up unexpectedly that moment, like they probably liked to do. He sat down at the edge of his chair. Make yourself comfortable, i said, uncomfortable myself with his uneasiness. i just want to talk with you. i only have a few more questions i'd like answered.

He shook so much i felt sorry for him. His big hand kept

feeling for his heart. Maybe he thought it was going to jump out or stop without his knowing. Do you remember a woman, i asked, and told my mother's name. He shook his head. He was so upset he probably couldn't think clearly enough to remember. Sure you do, i said. You must. She looked a lot like me. I don't know any Mexican women, he said. No, none that you socialized with publicly, i smiled calmly. None that your good wife ever knew about. He was still trembling, but his eyes flinched so that i knew he knew what i was getting at. Maybe, though, he still didn't know which one of them i was talking about.

So i showed him the chain with the pearls and gold locket that now fit around my wrist. Miss, I don't know what this is about, but I am going to call the police . . . he said, his old body wanting to get up and get to the telephone despised me, because there was a time when he could have easily overpowered me, knocked the gun out of my hand, twisted my arm until i fell on my knees and begged him to forgive my audacity. i saw it all in the twitching of his eyes and the corners of his thin mouth, how he hated me, had started out with just tolerance of my presence in his house and now hated me, not because i was his daughter, or that i reminded him of a woman he had abused in another time in his life, but just because i was there, pointing a gun at him and he had heard so many similar stories of intruders slyly getting entrance into decent citizens' homes, killing them mercilessly, ransacking their houses, making off with the shoeboxes of crisp bills neatly stacked away.

My mother? Who was she, but some Mexican whore with almond-shaped eyes and a fine tush he liked to pat when no one was looking. So she got pregnant? That was her problem. His eyes darted from the gun to the telephone.

Don't call the police, Old Man, i said, feeling the same

process of emotions, from feeling nothing to an intense hatred, but not enough to waste him, a hate that went from his little bungalow all up and down each one of those identical little houses throughout the entire neighborhood.

He got up and i got up. Since i didn't want to get close enough to where he might take the gun from me, i cocked it to stop him from picking up the phone. Then he gasped. Both his hands were over his chest and as he turned to see if i was going to shoot, i saw how his eyes bulged. Then he fell back, knocking over a small table with a huge, gaudy lamp in the shape of a geisha. It was useless. Either the man was faking it or really having a heart attack. i put the gun away and picked up my things. Do you want me to call the police, i asked. Do you want me to call a doctor? He just lay there on the gold carpeting right over the wet spot and gasped up at me. i left.

Two blocks down i pulled up at a gas station and called the emergency number to send an ambulance over to his house. Don't want that on my conscience, i said to myself, and went home.

He'll come after you and kill you, if he lived, my mother warned. He's a mean man. I don't know why you had to go over there in the first place; she pulls out a hanky from her apron pocket to blow her nose.

i never liked that place anyway. That's really why we decided to come back to this city. The one where everything happened/happens. The one movie directors love so much.

⊲ Vatolandia

Nobody understands Sara Santistevan. The truth is that Sara herself would be hard-pressed to explain Sara Santistevan. Not that she feels inclined to do that, leaving that kind of stuff to the pseudo-Freudianos around town and revering her dreams as other lives she is living too, so that she doesn't heed los Yungianos either. And let me tell you, even in a town like this one, you'll find Freudianos and Yungianos.

But for three years, since she moved here, she's become more and more of a recluse. It's not like Sara doesn't know how to have fun, neither, big beautiful bronze woman that she is! Nobody moves on the dance floor like Sara and nobody holds her liquor like her and nobody works as hard, and basically, nobody can do nothin' like Sara Santistevan does it. But she just doesn't talk to anybody anymore. Get it?

Now, I ain't saying here that she used to sleep around, okay? I'm not trying to imply anything about her that isn't true, 'cause I ain't like that. But it's not like she was the Immaculate Conception either, and with four kids, you know she must've slept with someone sometime which is what she doesn't do anymore and that is why nobody understands Sara.

Well, the first few months she was here you might have found her at Chacón's Bar or closing up the Colorado Lounge, maybe with just a comadre, or on a date with some vato, him buying her drinks and spinning her around fast and fancy-like to a two-step or a ranchera and she, getting pissed off finally because he got her all dizzy-like and made her look drunk or something out there in front of everybody.

When she moved here her kids were grown up already; the two youngest, in their teens finishing up high school, were staying with their father in Texas, is what she said. "All my exes are in Texas," is something else she liked to say, too, like the song, you know? ¡Ay, qué Sara! She's too much, man.

When she first moved up here from Lubbock, she bought herself un ranchito, some chickens, goats, even a couple of pigs. She does all right. At least it doesn't seem to be a problem for her to make ends meet. But I guess teachers make decent lana anyway, her being the chemistry teacher at the high school and all. Would you believe it?

She's the one who replaced Mr. Tafoya after that big mitote when he got caught with one of his students after school doing more than just cleaning the erasers. You remember. A vato chemistry teacher. Que cabrón.

But after that first winter Sara stopped going out. Nobody saw her around hardly, just maybe at the grocery store, or at the bank, or at the package liquor store picking up a six-pack. She wasn't hanging around with any of her new comadres. You'd just see her after school or on weekends running errands, driving by alone in her troquita, picking up feed for the animals. And with her just giving you a quick wave and wearing those dark glasses, it was impossible to tell anything.

Like, who was Sara, anyway, big-hipped woman who gets

up in the mornings to feed her pigs and milk the goats before going off to teach fifteen-year-olds chemistry. And she must be doing a good job of that too, since the school ain't been blown up yet . . .

That's a joke, all right?

Still this is what I have heard—what I was told by some reliable sources and you can take it or leave it, but you seem interested in la Sara, so I'll tell you what I know, and you can do whatever you want with it. Just leave me out of it:

When Sara first moved to town *everybody*, and I do mean EVERYBODY, wanted to get to know her. You know what I mean? Well, it's not like we get new people here all the time and it sure ain't like you get good-looking, available women who do all right for themselves, like Sara Santistevan. And let me add to all that, obviously smart, being a teacher and college educated and all. But see, here may be where the problem lies for Sara, 'cause *I* ain't all that sure that the smart part was considered by too many of the vatos around here as a good thing.

So like the vatos wanted to know her for obvious reasons and the comadres wanted to know her 'cause they just wanted to know her business. I'm sure there was one or two, especially at the high school, who really wanted to be friends with her. Those married goody-two-shoes types, you know the kind, who get a vicarious thrill from hearing about the life of a woman who doesn't listen to no one and doesn't have to, 'cause basically she ain't afraid of nothin', especially not of being alone. But anyway, little by little, maybe it went both ways, la gente started losing interest in Sara Santistevan and Sara Santistevan lost interest in the people around here, too.

A bunch of mitoteros in this town, nomas.

Now, Sara is about the age where you really can't tell exactly how old she is. She ain't no spring chicken, that's for sure;

and although you know she's been around the block a few times, her soles ain't all worn out yet so that you could say she probably got it in her to go around a few more times.

And *that's* just the kind of talk that probably started to get to Sara. It must have made her tired coming up with comebacks like "Tu abuela" to vatos who made those kinds of remarks to her, thinking they were flattering her or something. Saying things like "You're *still* a beautiful woman" and "You must've really had men going crazy over you . . . " Like she wasn't driving them crazy then and there. Mocosos.

But it's like some women just have something about them, some men do too, but we're talking about Sara here, so . . . young and old alike came around—like moscos—to make their play. From the bagboy down at the Martínez Supermarket to the clerks at the post office to the viejito who works in the booth at the bank parking lot, they all had something to say to Sara—in the beginning. Now, they only say things like "Will that be all, ma'am?" And don't even look her in the eye when they do.

What do you think she said to those vatos, anyway?

So finally, all this got to Sara so that she decided to classify the vatos who had come around—in order to make it easier to handle future vatos and to know what to do with the past vatos who might come around again ('cause some vatos are just like that, real necios, man); but basically she did it just to pass the time while she sipped on a beer one lonely Friday night after she had got done grading her students' tests and the expression "better alone than in bad company" had gained new meaning for her in recent times. For the time being, unless Jorge Negrete himself made a wrong turn down the road and rode up on his white horse to sweep her off her feet, Sara in Vatolandia figured she was better off as alone as the day that she was born.

Now, she called this list "The Sara Santistevan Vato Fan Club." She listed all the vatos who had dated her, slept with her, and even remotely fantasized about her (all the while acting like they weren't doing it, as if she couldn't tell by their sweaty palms and silly grins . . . like the viejito in the booth at the bank parking lot . . . then there was the baboso pushing the big broom around at the gym, lingering a long time on a little dirt watching Sara pump iron through the corners of his eyes).

Now, because they had been far too numerous for Sara to recall just off the top of her head, she divided this fan club into two chapters. Those over thirty-five years old she called the "Veterano Vatos" and those under thirty-five she called the "Junior Vatos."

If a vato was actually thirty-five when she met him, she would have had to put him in a group all by himself. But since she had never met one who said he was thirty-five right then, that was not a problem, and wouldn't be anyway, since all she would have to do then is call him "the thirty-five-year-old vato" and being the only one in that category, she would know right away who he was.

Sadly enough for Sara, all these vatos, the veterano vatos and the junior vatos rolled up altogether in a taco, wouldn't have served to fill one of Sara's molars. But in any case, she went on to try to recall them one by one, being bored and lonesome that night, like I said, and all the while wishing that Jorge Negrete on a white horse *would* ride by and sweep her away, but knowing that those things only happened to María Felix, she popped open another can of beer.

Plus, Jorge Negrete was dead anyway.

They just didn't make 'em like they used to, Sara must have thought wistfully. Although she wouldn't have said *no* to Andres García who was so fine at fifty that even her tío Noé back home said, while his wife was glued to the TV watching him on "El Magnate," that Andres García looked so good, *he'd* even go to bed with him! But Andres García had sixteen kids from at least as many women, so when it came down to it, Andres García was just another vato, only one with money—and the body of Dionysus. Check it out: a vato Dionysus.

When she actually thought about it, she wouldn't mind having a baby with Andres García. There were worse fates. Like the one with the man who did father her first two babies before she finished high school. The best thing she would say about the end of that story was that, although she had not said a word to that vato since 1977 when she left him for good, he had gotten real old-looking already. People tried to tell her, like, how much hair he had lost, and how he had got a front tooth punched out, and that he went around with a "plumber's butt," that is to say, his pants were all hanging low and shit so that his crack showed everytime he bent down. (Yeah, women talk like that too, now, among themselves, comparing vatos and making fun of 'em and basically, there's just no stopping them anymore. Even the married ones.)

Then one day before she left Lubbock, she found out that it was all true when she ran into him in a restaurant and she saw him for herself. He looked like he was in costume for a play, acting himself as an old man. His eyebrows were all wiry and his beard was almost white; he even had some long hairs coming out of his nose, and him just barely forty. He had been the best-looking vato in his senior class in high school, too.

"God punished him," Sara would say. "He made him old for being mean." Some vatos can be really mean, too. Like he didn't let her have anything to do with her family those five years they were together, calling her mother a Nazi and saying all her relatives wanted to do was brainwash Sara into leaving him.

In between the two husbands, Sara went and got her G.E.D. and then went to school at night and got her teaching degree. She really got a lot of satisfaction when people would go back and tell that first husband of hers how well she was doing, that she was going to college and all that. And no thanks to him, she would add, 'cause if it had been up to that vato, she'd have nothing but canas and varicose veins to show for herself, and be looking even older than him.

Now, I think that for the purposes of this telling I'll change the stories a bit and will use different names altogether, since I don't want any vatos accusing me of bad-mouthing them; and anyway a vato is a vato, so one way or another, you'll get the gist of the fiascos and fracasos Sara has gone through with the vatos in this town. And I want to add, just for the record, that *I* was not one of them. Like I said, this is what I *heard* and I ain't got nothing else to say but that.

At first Sara figured that chronologically would be the easiest way to make up her list, since nothing about any single vato set him apart enough to take precedence in being listed first.

There was just one among all those vatos that she had gotten to really like and he had only been passing through town that spring break . . . Let's just say he was the Mr. Mystery Vato who stole Sara's heart for a minute. Which was more than we could say for all the other vatos, most of whom could not even get to the buttons on her blouse much less to her heart.

She never did get to ask that vato his age. She had been too busy enjoying the smell of his skin and the way he held the tip of her tongue between his teeth when she tried to pull away from a kiss, and thinking after that very first night together that maybe he might decide to stay, but before she knew it, he was gone, just like he said he would be. He may have been the thirty-five-year-old vato in his own category; in his own category he was for sure, Sara thought. But ni modo, the vato was long gone and relegated to the annals of Sara's vato memoirs.

After him, it was funny 'cause what came to Sara's mind about several of the vatos was not how bad they had tried to make her feel—like she wasn't an able-bodied and able-minded woman, nor as smart, as sexy, as together as she was—and that little by little, sure as shootin', each was out to bring her down by pointing out things about her that he didn't like: the new way she was wearing her hair for instance, or that her favorite "Red-Red" lipstick was too red, or how she kissed him in bed, or when after she read a new "self-healing" book she was excited about and tried to talk about it with the current vato in her life, his lame excuse for discussion was to say something like, "You've just contradicted what you said a moment ago," like pointing out a contradiction meant that Sara was stupid and really hadn't understood at all what she had read, so why show off about it, and that, either way, she was not as smart as the vato who was quick to point all that out. And the real point to all that was—as if Sara hadn't been smart enough to see through it—was not the hair, the lipstick, nor that her kisses had anything to do with the vato not being able to get it up in bed, but that just like with her first husband, all those vatos wanted was to simply bring her down.

Sara doesn't like to be caught with nothing to say to these vatos when their time is up (if you knew her for five minutes you'd know that she carries handy comebacks like dimes to drop in the parking meter), but once, after a vato put her on the spot with that contradiction thing, she remembered a line from her favorite poet. Walt Whitman was really the only poet she had ever read, in night school in a required English course, but ese Whitman had just about said it all for her, so she went back to him again and again. Remembering this— and you have to keep in mind, Sara doesn't necessarily enjoy giving verbal cachetadas, but some vatos just ask for it—she said to the vato, and I *quote* (since I ain't no stranger to Walt Whitman either): "Do I contradict myself? Very well, then I contradict myself. (I am large, I contain multitudes.)"

Now, in the case of a more intelligent vato, he would have known when he was licked and taken defeat graciously, but instead this one had to show the quality of what he was made, which is to say not very high-grade, so he came right back with something like, "Yeah, baby doll, I can see you're *large*." And I'm sure he wouldn't like to know that her last and only memory of him was of him standing there looking up all stupid-like at Sara with that cocky grin he was so proud of, since that was the last time she laid eyes on him, sending him out of her house that very next minute and not even turning around to watch him leave.

No, none of these unpleasant memories came to mind first when she summed up the unsavory essence of their recollection in total—since Sara didn't like to hold on to the kind of bad stuff some people enjoy putting on a woman who is only trying hard to be happy and, anyway, anyone who only wanted to make himself look good at the expense of Sara's self-confidence was quickly out of her life, like the vato I just mentioned. No, what came to her mind right away, that is, the residue of her experience with them altogether, was simply that these vatos were all short vatos.

Which brought up the possibility of yet another category, which she quickly dismissed, because if there came to be a short vato category, that would imply that there would have to be a big vato category. And the truth of it was that Sara didn't consider any vato big enough to be put under any kind of "big" category, even if it was just 'cause of the size of his hat.

Now, Sara, as we both know, is a little taller than a lot of women and a lot bigger all the way around, although you could never say she had anything out of place or too much of it. Some women are just like that. They got a lot and it looks like it should all be there. And she didn't have any hang-ups about occasionally being with a little man. Which again tells you what kind of woman esa Sara is.

Considering herself a tolerant woman and a woman with a sense of humor, she let them go around in their bikini briefs getting in karate stances, making those controlled breathing noises and showing how bad they were, trying to assure her that if the occasion ever arose, they would be her hero.

However, sometimes a small man trying to compensate for his littleness overdoes it and no kind of "attitude adjustment" in any bar from any vato who is all too happy to straighten the little dude out ever helps. Those little boogers just don't learn, do they? What ends up happening is that the vato exercises his delusions of grandeur on unsuspecting women, like gabachas who don't know any better, or homegirls who ain't got no choice—neither of which Sara happens to be.

But like I said, Sara wasn't interested in figuring out the why of things or of people when they were mean to her. She had done all that after her first husband, who had surely been the biggest cabrón she'd ever meet.

If she was unhappy, she had learned to eliminate the source of the unhappiness, like taking a pair of garden clippers, snip, crack, y ya, which sometimes in itself was a thing that still made her unhappy, but not for long. After all, she figured, the road to "self-healing" was a thorny and bristly one, indeed.

Sara's list might have started out like this:

The Sara Santistevan Vato Fan Club

Veterano Vatos	Junior Vatos
Leroy	Junior
José	Vatos
Hilario	Richard

These were vatos who were just too small for Sara. She did not have a run of small men, you understand, she had let go of the chronological idea for the spontaneous one of how these vatos all came to mind at once. The thing about it was that Sara did not reject them because they were small, nor because she had to hunch a little when two-stepping cheek-to-cheek or to accommodate the difference in their proportions at other more delicate moments, because if that was the point, she wouldn't have gone out with them in the first place—except for Hilario. She did admit that she rejected Hilario flat-out because he was just too little (*and* because by then she had gotten wise to short vatos so she could tell already that ese Hilario thought of himself as a don Chingoncito, if not a don Chingón).

But one thing is to be arrogant and rude and another is to be arrogant and rude strutting around a woman's house in your little snakeskin boots and your little Western-style shirt with mother-of-pearl buttons and your sad little butt in tight size-slim jeans that have a faded line where the crease is always anal retentively ironed, and your Christmas aftershave slapped on your little hairless jaw and you believin' you are the biggest chingón in town because you got yourself a woman like Sara.

And not for long, neither. Since as soon as you start trying to tell Sara about herself, like how she didn't mend the fence right for the animals but you ain't surprised, since how could *she* know—and you both knowing what that implied, or telling her to do things for you like, get me a beer, honey, would you?, or complaining 'cause the Rocky Hernandez concert cost too much, so you and she weren't going—*you* were the one that was gone—out of her life and so fast, it took you six months before you realized it.

(And don't think she didn't go to hear Rocky Hernández without you, neither. Pichicate vato.)

There were no married vatos for Sara. And this was no coincidence. A wedding band or the traces of one having been just taken off, leaving a light ring mark, a foto in his wallet when he opened it to pay for the taco he had just bought for her ("Let's do lunch," some vatos have the nerve to say), just a casual reference to an "old lady" and the philandering vato was out. As if a vato announcing he was married could ever be taken as a casual reference, although some vatos, believe it or not, try to pull it off, saying something like, "My wife and I don't really get along but we stay together because of the kids" or "because of our families" or "because we got married by the Church." Yeah, vatos are still trying to get away with those lines. And some do, because unfortunately, there are a lot of lonely women out there. That was enough for Sara. Nothing more pesado than a vato casado. Huh, ese?

But though she escaped the vatos casados, there had been a few baggy-assed divorced vatos unfortunately that slipped past her married-vato screening process. Sara wasn't interested in divorced vatos neither. She wasn't interested in their child support payments and their truck payments and the mortgage on the house that they didn't live in no more, nor in their khakis that they couldn't iron right themselves now that their wives weren't around to do it for them, nor that they had never learned how to heat up a tortilla; and she sure wasn't interested in them falling asleep right after their five-minute lovemaking. Worse than a vato casado, she concluded, was a vato cansado.

So, undoubtedly, Sara's list grew to something like this:

The Sara Santistevan Vato Fan Club

Veterano Vatos	Junior Vatos
Leroy	Richard
José	Benito
Hilario	
Loreto	
José M.	

¡Hijola! The vatos repeated themselves—kind of like when you eat reheated adovado. That's why I put the surname initial of the second José (even though we know I'm not using real names here, all right?), since José M. was sure no chaparito and should not be mistaken for one of the short vatos. José M. was a big ol' dude, who breeded Arabian horses and raised cattle and came pretty close to making Sara think twice about living alone, but then he started talking about his ex–old lady, like every time that he and Sara got together and finally, she just got tired of it all and told the vato that the next Saturday night maybe he should spend it with his ex-wife talking about Sara for a change.

There was one veterano vato who Sara finally figured out must have been gay. I tell you, it's so hard for some vatos to admit that they are really a vato's vato . . . and got no business with a lady. So, for trying to mess with Sara's mind because of his being in a state of denial about himself, he'd most surely go on the list (or at least he'd go on *mine* if I had a list):

Bernardo

Aw man—I've forgotten to mention a whole bunch of the junior vatos! But that's just how junior vatos were for la Sara, not enough there, really, to linger with a real woman for very long. They were always doing things out of step as if their motor skills weren't fully developed yet. Like, sometimes they tried to kiss her when she was in the middle of a sentence or chewing something, so anxious they were to get down to business before she might realize that they were just a "mocoso," wasting her time and eating her food, and would kick them out.

Then again, some junior vatos never tried to kiss her at all because they just had too much respect for her, or worse, 'cause although they were attracted to her, they couldn't see themselves getting involved with a woman "her age." And *those* vatitos, most of whom were still tied to their mothers' apron strings—going home to eat their mother's food, to have her wash their clothes, that is, if they had moved out at all— she did not need around for sure, she decided pretty quick.

We'll add three of them to Sara's list (three being kind of a lucky number for some people, even if those vatitos were not too lucky):

Benjamín
Antonio
Roger (Rogelio)

And as if the obvious were too much to have thought of right away, what's say we talk a little bit about the *real* veter- ano vatos that strayed past Sara's way:

Henry
Elvis
Faustino

That is, the vatos de Vietnam. Now, it happened that for some time just hearing that a vato had been in Vietnam, twenty years ago or not, set off a little warning signal in Sara's head. Back in those days when they first came back, Sara was already married, so she didn't have to experience them personally. But still, she heard stories through friends, for instance, how at a family get-together, all of a sudden the Vietnam vato would go off and start throwing things around and beating up on his mother. Things like that.

Anyone can only imagine what those vatos went through in Vietnam. At seventeen or nineteen years old they went off, leaving their little villages and barrios, kissing la Mary Sue or la Debbie goodbye and coming back to give Mary Sue and Debbie a life of hell because they could not shake those six months in the Vietcong jungle.

The thing about a Vietnam vato that Sara Santistevan learned right away was that he does not trust no one. When a Vietnam vato looks you dead in the eye and says he doesn't even trust his abuela, believe him. She respected what a Vietnam vato went through, but she kept away from him.

Still, maybe 'cause it was over twenty years ago and a vato would hesitate to mention it right away, and for sure, would most likely go through the divorced-vato screening process first, every now and then, Sara ended up going out with a vato not knowing that he was a Vietnam veterano, like Faustino. And who would have guessed about his short fuse, being the soft-spoken man that he was. I mean, *I* don't know Faustino myself; I just heard all this, you understand, but I've known vatos like him, and it's a sad set of circumstances indeed.

But there they were, having a club sandwich at a twenty-four-hour pancake joint after they had been out dancing, having a few drinks, and basically having a getting-to-know-each-other good time, when out of the blue, he started complaining that she wasn't listening to him.

She made a little apology and went on eating but he went off on her anyway, claiming she had no respect for him. Without having to figure it all out Sara knew pretty much right away what was happening. The veterano was losing control. Meanwhile, all she wanted to do was finish her club sandwich, get out her car keys, and say "Adios amigo," just like that French singer said on that cassette tape, that the traveling Mr. Mystery Vato left with her as the only material memento she had of their ever-so-tenuous but true love. Sara didn't get any of the lyrics of that old cabaret music except when the woman said "Adios amigos," and since you could hear a loud foghorn in the background along with the bandoleon, she figured the singer was saying goodbye to some sailorboys just as cool as a woman without compromise and commitment could be, which I'm sure is just how Sara wanted to make her exit at that moment: cool and without compromise.

But the next thing Sara knew, the vato was crying. Not big ol' sobs, you understand, but his eyes were all red, him gritting his teeth, you know, the way a vato cries. Well, she would have wanted to join him, not really knowing what else to do and kind of thinking that that's what a woman does when a vato cries, is cry with him. The rum-and-Cokes she had that night could've helped her squeeze out a few tears, plus thinking about how this vet vato was on the verge of ruining the whole night and she might as well have stayed home altogether if it was all going to lead to a bad drama at a brightly lit diner at three in the morning, but the coffee and her sandwich, along with the vato's rude behavior, had already sobered her up, so she focused on her sandwich like a Buddhist with a mantra and said nothing.

Seeing himself ignored, Faustino pulled himself together.

He asked the waitress for her pen and on a paper napkin he explained to Sara about post-traumatic shock syndrome. Yep, she thought, he's got that right, 'cause for sure she was being sobered up, if not shocked by some kind of syndrome—since she knew enough to know that whatever was transpiring in his mind had nothing to do with her. She let the waitress pour her some more coffee and while she was mixing in the cream and sugar, she saw that he was getting annoyed 'cause it looked to him again like she wasn't paying attention. He threw the pen down. "Never mind," he said.

"No, no," she said, "go on, show me what you wanted to show me."

He picked up the pen again and wrote: S. O. R. C. "S" stood for situation, "O" for organism response, "R" for reaction or response, and "C" for consequence. He had skipped the "R" part with her, he said, letting his body respond before letting himself assimilate the situation long enough to react appropriately.

And that was the only time she went out with Faustino de Vietnam.

Ah! But how could I forget to mention Mister Flowers— "que siempre le hechaba la flor," as they say down ol' Méjico way, always with a pretty word to flatter her! The vato poet: ageless and sometimes alcoholic, but always in pursuit of the ultimate communion with his god, his universe, his ultimate and final truth. And Sara . . . Sarita was an oh so brief sigh of inspiration in that wretched vato's existence . . . She was also good for a free meal whenever he dropped in on her and even for a small loan occasionally whenever he (always with a grand expression of regret and embarrassment, of course) hit on her for one.

Such small prices for a woman to pay in exchange for worship and complete devotion, so the vato poet tried to make her think. The second time he came by, uninvited if not unexpected, he took off his dog-earred Stetson and bowed to her, kissing Sara's callused hand and pledging his faithfulness and eternal debt to her simply for having—with her mere existence—given him the reassurance that such beauty and tenderness in this miserable world could be found. If he had survived untold hardships for any reason, he told her, it was for the sole purpose of serving her, to be her personal penitente. His Santa Sara.

But even a saint has a bad day now and then, and on such a one, in Sara's straight kind of speech that has nothing florid or lyrical about it but being so down to earth is beautiful in its own way, I can bet she looked at him with that right eyebrow of hers that goes up like this, and said something like: "Mister Flowers . . . " (Mister Flowers she called him but his name was Leonard. Sara was the only person who ever called that vato Mister.) "Mister Flowers," Sara may have said, "talk is cheap."

For all his profuse declarations of romantic love and carnal desire, he had never made love with Sara—the crucial fact about all this being that it wasn't 'cause he hadn't had the chance. Y'know what I mean, ese?

So when the ageless vato poet wasn't busy talking (which Sara figured out soon enough was *all* that he could do), she suspected he was busy expending the rest of his energy trying to scam good women who kept a fresh pot of beans on the stove and a little free-flowing petty cash in the till. So Sara wasn't impressed. Not even with the crumpled photocopy of a not-so-terse verse he had published once in some obscure, no-longer-in-print rag out of San Francisco.

Just like she wasn't impressed with the pseudo–Native American peyote-chewing sweat lodge vatos with their constant proselytizing about the advanced ways of peoples that nobody would want to argue were not better than those who had been governing the planet for too long. But what Sara Santistevan did take offense at with regards to all their going on about things (Sara, who had been struggling since day one to make sense of life and society for just one moment, knowing that something was definitely set askew long before her birth, because she just *knew* it) was how they talked to her, as if she didn't know what she knew. As if (like with those plants and animals that were being made extinct because of greed and ignorance) without the control (disguised as protection and enlightenment) of the politically correct sensitive-male spiritual indigenist vato and without his self-righteous understanding of what her place in the schema of the cosmos should be, *she* would also become extinct. Dream on, vatos of the Wannabe Tribe.

'Cause although Sara Santistevan may not look no different to a vato than any other fry-bread-eating tortilla-rolling mother of four, twice-divorced homegirl statistic, get this: she has not only heard of the theory of relativity, she *understands* it. More importantly, Sara knew that before there was sun worship the moon ruled. Ho!

Anyway, there were vatos whose names she never even knew and therefore would not be able to list, although they definitely belonged there. Like the one who worked at the post office downtown. That vato flirted with EVERY female who went in there. It was a worse feeling for Sara than walking into the Colorado Lounge. A woman couldn't go in there with her neatly wrapped packages to her mother and kids in Lubbock, and needing stamps to mail all her bills, without being stared down and made to wish suddenly that she hadn't come in there wearing her sweats and should have put some lipstick on.

He used to say things to Sara, despite the sweats and sweaty

T-shirts, until he found out through a package she was returning that she was a chemistry teacher. "Ah, a lady scientist, uh?" he said. To which she should have responded—what? "Ah, a vato post office clerk, uh?" But instead she gave him a look that amounted to the same thing, stuck her chin in the air, and walked out.

And you know there ain't nothing a vato detests more than a woman's cold-blooded rejection. He can go around acting like Antonio Aguilar, king of the rodeo, convinced that every woman around town would only welcome the chance to be with him for one night, but let a woman get on her high horse with him when he pays the slightest bit of attention to her—as if she were so beautiful or something—and she becomes the immediate and unpardonable target of his contempt.

The truth is some vatos out there have their own lists, bien chingones that they are. Written on prison walls, tattooed on their arms, in their little black books and Rolodexes, in their receipt pads that their wives don't see, their yellow legal pads at work, on special computer programs, on the backs of business cards and in matchbooks: "Women Who Make Their Lives Misery and Hell for the Sake of Your Love"—and "Women You Just Don't Mess With." But those women who make the second list, instead of getting a vato's respect for knowing enough not to let him mess with her or even try to, are not only subjected to the vato's downright hostility, they may as well be dead.

There's no shaking hands and calling it a tie, a matter of irreconcilable differences or a conflict of interests, just saying they could at least be friends even if nothing more. Being a man about it, in other words (and I still ain't naming no names here, okay?).

No, as soon as Sara sent a vato on his way, she got him bad-mouthing her around town. He'd be drinking a beer with friends down at Chacón's and telling them how much he left her wanting him.

So if she got a flat tire on a dark road one night—because she had not put up with his showing up late all the time (especially 'cause he couldn't get away earlier from his old lady), or because she refused to go with him to his boss's retirement party for the sake of impressing somebody, or because she never dressed up for him in a froufrou nightgown like he hinted at a few times—she had better not think of calling him. A vato ain't got no use for a woman who does not know that he is *the* vato, the Texas Tornado himself— Tigres del Norte watch out! Aw, baby, don't you know? *Nobody* messes with a vato! And that's why nobody in Vato-landia understands Sara Santistevan.

◁ JUAN IN A
MILLION

What Mercedes brought back from her youthful travels were all the colors she had seen, especially in Malaysia, she said, where the sunset was an incandescent kaleidoscope.

Italy, her first stop, because it was the cradle of Renaissance art, of course she loved. It was as if she'd stepped into her art books.

In Paris she made her living painting on the Champs Elysées. She did only portraits, never caricatures. She loved Paris, too, in a different way, and the summer she spent near Cannes with Michel, whom she met while she worked as an au pair for his friends. She learned to speak French as one should, she often said, with a lover.

In Japan—amog her various destinations throughout Asia— she worked for a while as a hostess in the *American Doll Bar*. She used the handful of English words she retained from prep school in her native Mexico. The Japanese clientele didn't mind her crooked English so heavily spiced with Spanish intonations. On the other hand, she did mind the clientele, and that job did not last. Nevertheless, before leaving Japan, she managed to find and work with Madame Funo, one of the greatest textile artists alive. Her mentor, seeing a young woman who had traveled so far and who obviously had talent but was broke, did not charge her for lessons.

In Spain, which actually came before Japan, Mercedes had parted with her longtime boyfriend who had been the one who convinced her to travel to Europe in the first place. Along with him went their original itinerary, the quasi-protection of a male companion, and her ticket home.

Mercedes was twenty-four, not long out of art school in Mexico City. She wrote to her widowed father and he sent his only daughter enough to buy a return ticket. Instead, Mercedes invested in Guatemalan textiles, which, she was told by a very reliable source, were selling quite well at *El Rastro*, the famous Madrid flea market.

That was where she met José Antonio, eight years ago.

It was a cold January Sunday, and Mercedes put out her colorful wares: bags, sashes, wallets, friendship bracelets, all woven in cobalt blue, canary yellow, and brick red on hand looms by small Mayan women who worked with calloused fingers and feet hours on end far away for pennies. For more than pennies, Mercedes had purchased an acquaintance's entire stock but she was confident she could sell it all in one Sunday.

"How much is the vest?", the young man with a cigarette clutched between thin lips called out, his breath visible from the cold and smoke. What? Mercedes started to say, but looking down, realized quickly he was asking about her own Guatemalan vest. It was the only vest in stock and because of the chilly weather she'd put it on. "It's not for sale," she told him. She smiled. Mercedes had a smile that could sell anything. "Buy something else from me—don't be mean!" she said flirtatiously.

"No, no, it's the vest that I want!" the young man said. "No deal," she said. And she went on with her day, selling out most but not all of her merchandise. And the young man with a pale face and eyelashes like two luscious centipedes kept coming back and insisting on the vest. As the sun went down, he helped her gather up her things, load them in her traveler's size backpack, insisting all the while on the sale.

"José Antonio," he told her his name as she was saying: No, thanks, good-bye, and very nice to meet you. . . . "Name your price, please! *Vale*?" he persisted.

Mercedes stared. He looked like (and as it turned out, was) a college student. She felt wise beyond her years compared to him, a woman of the world (and this was before her three-year stint traveling alone throughout Asia!), and sized up the persistent tenderfoot. Men! Men get what they ask for, she thought to herself—for the first time but not the last since. And she named a price that was without question—too much.

José Antonio did not balk and instead pulled out his wallet and paid for the vest, which she took off immediately seeing he was serious.

How serious a man José Antonio was who went after what he wanted Mercedes didn't know until eight years later, when she found herself doing freelance work in Chicago and her father forwarded a letter that had come to her from Madrid. Inside the envelope, with a lovely greeting from José Antonio, was a recent photo of him wearing the vest she had sold him.

He had given her his address that day at the flea market and while she was traveling she sent him a postcard with her family's address. That, too, was years ago.

José Antonio now ran the family business, he wrote, and could not get away but he'd be enchanted if he heard from her, he said. It all seemed rather sudden after so long, but Mercedes finally decided, why not? Along with a postcard

(Mercedes was not very good at writing) she sent him a picture of herself in a sari taken with some women in India, another of herself in a bikini taken by the French boyfriend on the beach, and a third of herself in front of her grand-prize-winning painting last spring in Mexico City.

José Antonio started calling; as persistently as he had wanted that vest, he suddenly wanted Mercedes. He always called at around three in the morning because of the time difference and because Mercedes didn't mind. She rather liked being awakened by a passionate male voice, although she wan't crazy about his accent, she told him, which for some reason came off as arrogant.

He offered to send her a ticket to Madrid since he couldn't get away from work. She would think about it, she said, maybe in the summer when she could get away; but privately she started making plans to take advantage of the free passage and start traveling again.

Then, out of the blue, Michel called. She had traveled *twice* from Mexico to see him in France and *twice* she had left with her pride and heart chopped in two like avocado halves with a nasty black pit popping out. Michel was not a marrying man, he had told her. He was twelve years older than she and set in his ways, she decided. Of all things, years later, Michel had changed his mind. She hadn't seen him in years. What's with men? she thought. I'll never ever understand them, she concluded. Now, a little older and having learned a thing or two, she really did believe herself a worldly-wise, sophisticated woman, which meant she knew enough to know now that she didn't know it all. "You can't come to see me, I'm living with someone," she told Michel and stopped taking his calls. The phone rang at all hours. She knew it was Michel, although he didn't leave a message. Finally, one day he said on the machine. "Pick up, Mercedes. I know you're there and I know you don't live with any man!"

She consented reluctantly to let Michel visit her in Chicago, persuaded by his invitation to take her to New York for a few weeks.

One night José Antonio called. "Guess what?" He had managed to get a week off from work and was coming to see her. "I almost got in a traffic accident today," he said. "And all I could think of was that I could not let anything happen to me before I saw you again."

Well, she couldn't very well say no after having been told that, except that the week he proposed to fly to the States was exactly when Michel would be there. "You don't want to come out to Chicago in spring," she told the Madridian, thinking it prudent not to tell him about Michel yet. "It's colder than your winters. You'll freeze to death."

He didn't argue and they made plans for summer. So it was all set. First a visit from Michel, then one from José Antonio.

Maybe, just maybe she wouldn't grow old alone, she thought. Meanwhile, as the days warmed up, on weekends and sometimes weeknights Mercedes had fun smooching at the night clubs she went to, mostly to dance, because she loved to dance. Those young men were nothing to take seriously, she told her friends. They gave her rides around town, took her out to eat. All were named Juan to make keeping track easier. Most worked in *taquerías* and restaurants, but some were also artists like her. No matter how tongues wagged and rumors flew, none were ever invited up to her studio, she said. The old man who served as a night watchman in her building could have testified to that.

All spring and when early summer blossomed, it was he who greeted her every night when she was dropped off by the evening's dancing partner. "You sure have a lot of boyfriends," he said one night.

"No, the Juans are just friends!" she laughed, because the evening had gone well and she was in a good mood. She had also had two margaritas, which was her limit and which left her feeling dizzy but happy.

"Oh, I see! You lookin' for Juan in a million!" the old man kidded in his Russian accent, trying to make a joke.

"Yes!" she laughed, but not getting it as he pressed the elevator button for her. He always made sure she got on safely before going up, up in the rickety contraption that never failed to scare her a bit all the way to the ninth floor. Her studio faced east and she got the most marvelous light to paint by, thanks to the building supervisor who moved her up there from the fourth floor facing the dark north when she gave notice that she was going to have to move out because of such bad lighting. He didn't even charge her the higher rent that went with the higher apartment with the better light because he said he wanted to support the arts.

One hot afternoon in June Mercedes ran into the building supervisor in the elevator, who gave her some bad news. The old watchman had died on a much-anticipated fishing trip the weekend before. Mercedes was shocked. The old man seemed so well, so content. She wiped her eyes. "By the way," the supervisor said, "he left something for you. I'll leave it in your mailbox." Mercedes was surprised and, later, more surprised when she found the envelope the old watchman left. In it was a handwritten letter in which he declared his love for her. He had never married, he said. He wanted her to have his savings. It was in the envelope, too.

Death was a peculiar place from which to get a letter, Mercedes thought. But it was nice to know there was a limit as to how far away a man could be before he let her know how he felt about her. With her unexpected inheritance, to start with, she bought a pair of white, open-toed sandals. On the same day, she also bought a roll of fine linen canvas and six sable brushes to begin a new series of self-portraits, waiting for Michel. Then for José Antonio.

◁ AGAIN, LIKE BEFORE

This city belongs to us. It was the first thought I had when we landed. It belongs to us despite the hard rain and the fact that I have been locked in my hotel room all evening. I stare out of the window, at the rain, and listen to my "neighbors" in the room next door discussing something very important in Chinese or in Vietnamese or in some other language beyond the range of my meager comprehension of communication.

I left you a message on your machine two hours ago.

I did not think of this as your city until we landed. It was still daylight but the rain made it hard to see your city, the streets that you see everyday. After I got my room I leaned against the doorway for a while since it was stuffy inside. A Hindu delivery man walked past me with a pizza for the people next door. He eyed me up and down. I smiled at him, I don't know why. After he delivered his pizza he eyed me again as he passed me once more and just as he was about to turn the corner he stopped and turned back. "How much?" he asked me. He was standing objectionably close, close enough to smell his pores. "What?" I said.

"How much?" he repeated.

Understanding then what he meant, I turned away from him. I was repulsed. "You'd better hurry along," I said without looking at him, "my husband's on his way."

He hesitated as if he knew I was lying, but then decided that "no" was no for whatever reason, so he did as I asked. I looked down at my dress. Perhaps it was too short, the décolletage too revealing. My hair, perhaps. All of me, too . . . No, I dismissed the thoughts, the excuses, that is, that society gives a woman for such unsavory encounters.

I remember when you made my hair up just like yours. By chance, when we met our hair was the same length, cut the same, long layers of curls. Mine were from a permanent, yours were natural. After our shower and shampoo you applied globs of sticky stuff from aerosol canisters to make my hair stiff and full like yours. You dressed me in your expensive clothes. We went out that night. There was a *gentlemen's club* you wanted to show me.

We were the only two females in the place. Two minutes after we sat at a table, a young man in an Armani suit leaned over from the next table and whispered to me, "Do you girls know what kind of place this is?"

Without looking at him, but staring in front of me, as I did with the Hindu pizza delivery man earlier, I responded, "Do you know what kind of girls we are?"

It was one of the worst evenings of my life. Well, not my life. But of my summer here with you. The entertainment for that evening was a chanteuse. Now there were three of us. A singer who sat on the piano and did her best with a repertoire of Broadway show tunes and in between told jokes that, of course, being a gay bar, had to be gay jokes. I don't know why

I say "of course," but you know that what God gave me in other ways He deprived me of with regards to a sense of humor. So as the evening progressed my bad mood grew worse. Seeing *us*, however, *together*, she could not resist the temptation and spontaneously improvised her whole performance at our expense. Did we have our hair done at a two-for-one? Were we *engaged*? She jumped off her piano and with mike in hand came over to us beneath a spotlight in the otherwise darkened room. "Excuse me, dear," she said, leaning over to me, "is that *aftershave* you have on?"

I grabbed her by the back of the neck and kissed her hard on the mouth. When she pulled back she tried to laugh it off but retreated to the safety of the piano telling the audience she would make sure she would sit in such a way that neither my "girlfriend" nor I could get a "view" under her dress.

When the show was over, you said, "Why did you say yes when she asked if we are engaged?"

"Why not?" I said. I finished my second and last drink. Two was my limit you said. Two drinks for me. None for you. The benefits one gets from being with someone who has already gone through recovery include involuntary recovery.

"But we're not," you said. You were pouting. The guy in the Armani and his friends were enjoying our argument. They eavesdropped on us, drank Moet & Chandon, and it was all great fun.

My second and last drink finished, the only other female in the whole place a misogynist, and you, mad because I didn't want to marry you—"Pay the bill," I said, and then, "I'll see you later." I got up and got my jacket from the coat and hat guy and went out to catch a cab.

It was our city, our summer, and I hated it. I can let myself remember now, sitting here listening to the rain, wondering if you will get in tonight and get my message, if you will call, and if I will care whether you do or not.

It was your money, your Greek Orthodox parents in the suburbs holding the purse strings, your gay brother who came to check up on you saw me there, and stayed.

Okay. He was only twenty-two, had never been with a man (not a woman either for that matter), and I have no right to assume he is gay. The fact that I walked into the dining room one evening and found him sitting on his married companion's lap trying to spoon-feed him I suppose was one of those cultural-difference things that he was always insisting that I didn't understand about you and your family.

By the same token the fact that he came in one afternoon with his married companion, while we were making love with the bedroom door open, was equally ignored. You know, one of those In-the-Afternoon-Greek things.

Now, IF you were, you know, like *that* . . . he would have had to beat you, again, as he had the year before when he suspected it. So, no, of course you weren't. And I? *I*? What was *I* doing there with you? I was part of the family, like his married friend whose wife apparently was still in Athens having a baby. We were all part of the family, until the end of summer.

If you don't call, I don't care, you know. But if you don't call I know it's only because you're away, on vacation with your family, perhaps. I know that everything here with you is the same. Everything. While the end of that summer caused a part of me to perforate and it ripped off as soon as I got on the plane. I took your credit card number that morning, called a travel agent, and made the reservation. While you were in class I was making my way to the airport. I thought of using your credit card number and charging a watch for myself at the airport but I did not because I am a fair person.

You were not.

You promised me a round-trip ticket but wouldn't let me go. And your punk brother saying hypocritically to me, "Stay, Celeste! Why do you want to go so soon?" Well, who had invited *him*? He came one weekend with his married friend and the two camped out in the living room permanently, or at least until I left. "Isn't that my sister's cross?" he asked, fingering the gold crucifix on the eighteen-karat-gold chain you had put around my neck that morning before you left for class and I was still half asleep in bed. "Yes," I said. Then added, "Your sister gave it to me this morning."

Surely he understood friendship, I thought. Hadn't he told us how he had spontaneously given his own watch to his married friend because he did not have one and could not afford it, being in this country all alone looking for work and his wife in Greece having a baby? Friendship. You know, like two guys who sleep embraced in the spoon position on the floor every night. One married, one looking for a wife. You know, friends.

"Get rid of these guys or I'm leaving," I demanded every night and every night you laughed. "He's my brother!" you said.

"There's something weird about all this," I insisted.

"What? Do you think my brother could be *gay*?" The thing was, you were *really* asking me. I didn't know what was going on. And it got more that way the evening a certain woman called you, a "friend of the family" as your brother referred to her because she spoke Greek, but you and I knew she was after you. Your brother took the call since you were in the shower. *"I know she wants to go out with me!"* he whispered to me with his hand over the mouthpiece. "Give me that!" I said. He pulled away, and with the telephone clutched to his chest, he ran into the bathroom and locked the door.

The next thing I knew he had given the phone to you while you were in the shower. I could hear you shouting over the water, "What? Who? Oh, hi! How are ya!"

The brother's married companion who didn't speak English was standing outside the door by then, both of us staring at it and hearing you and your brother talk, sometimes in English, sometimes in Greek, together and on the phone and laughing, and then it sounded like he too was taking a shower.

I asked you about that later. You said it was no big deal in your rather large family. Surely this was not a cultural misunderstanding. By this point I decided it was me and my own prudish upbringing where adult siblings were too uptight to bathe together.

No, that was not the reason I left without telling you. No, my darling whom I once desired so, at least for one summer, it wasn't two ostensibly straight men sleeping together on your living room floor and spoon-feeding each other at the table. It wasn't your brother coming into the bedroom without knocking and his friend always watching us from the doorway. It wasn't that we ate at some of the best restaurants in town but you always chose when and where and if we would go at all. It wasn't my two-drink limit. It wasn't the gifts you gave and took back when I wouldn't say I loved you, when I wouldn't say I'd marry you, when I wouldn't stay forever, in your apartment, in your city.

It wasn't how you always shut the lights out, got on your knees before a big framed picture of Jesus the Good Shepherd on the wall to say your prayers before getting into bed to make love with me.

And it wasn't those things about you and me there with you that summer that are too despicable to recall in this lifetime, but which will surely be recalled for us in some way in the afterlife for being so despicable and having nothing to do with love at all.

There it is. There's your call. I'll let it ring and you will surely call back again. And if I don't get out of here, sometime in the middle of the night you will come over here. You'll suspect I am out and you will wait in the lobby and hope to catch me. Catch me, as if I had surely been out committing a violation against you, my sin of insisting on existing without you.

If I don't move quickly, you will move even more so and there will be no escaping you. Perhaps I should get another room. Call a cab. Find an all-night bar. I can't stand the thought of it; you'll come and in minutes you'll be crying, making those little donkey-like noises when you start to hyperventilate and cause a scene. We'll be forced to get an ambulance and spend the night in an emergency room. Then your older brother, the doctor, will appear. And he'll see you, red and half-strangulated by your own mucus, and see me and ask no one in particular since you won't be able to answer, "Who's this?"

And I'll have to tell him and look away, repulsed by the fact that he doesn't care who I am but has asked simply to have better reason to dismiss me.

No, it's too much. I should never have let you know that I was here. After all, there was no reason to tell you. It was just that we landed and I was sucked up by the tentacles of this, your city, and your name and that summer that were all inseparable and I called as soon as I put my bag down on the bed in this room. You must have heard that I've married. That isn't *the* reason why I shouldn't have called but it is a reason why I shouldn't have called because you will surely reproach me for it.

You'll write something meant to make me feel terrible on

the bathroom mirror again in your crimson red lipstick just before you leave like, "Why did you ever bother to call in the first place???" And I'll spend an hour trying to wipe it all off so that the maid won't think badly of me tomorrow.

But how could she think badly of me when it is you who is capable of doing such things? Like going through my phone-book and ripping out all the pages with names of people you didn't know and who were therefore suspected of being romantic liaisons. No, that was not the reason I left you either.

I left you because I simply did not love you. I left you because I grew bored with your long, black eyelashes. I left you because your money was a nuisance in my life. Above all, summer had ended and I left because that is when I said I would leave, and I did.

Which is what I had better do now, again. Or perhaps not. It doesn't matter. If you want to come by, speeding in your little car in the rain, getting my room number, pounding on the UP button, then taking the stairs, do it. It is your night, your city, your money, your hotel for all I know. Nothing about you matters to me now. And all of this here, that I am in, is you, again, like before.

◁ A Kiss Errant

Kiss me," he said. It was easy to kiss him. One of the easiest things I ever did was to kiss him. I closed my eyes, drew my blood-red lips together, leaned over. Then he turned away. I landed in midair or rather the requested kiss went *poof*! in the air, the way love does sometimes.

"Why did you do that?" I asked.

"Because," he said, not looking at me, smiling but not smiling, loving me but not wanting to, "I just wanted to remember that at least one time I was able to resist you."

◁ WHAT BIG CITIES ARE FOR

"No I DO NOT MIND HEARING THE ENTIRE AUDIO OF *KEY LARGO* WHILE I AM TRYING TO MEDITATE—THANK YOU!" David shouted at the closed door which sealed off the parlor from the kitchen. He slapped each Voyager tarot card down on the kitchen table forming the Celtic spread and lit an unfiltered Camel cigarette. Ever since he heard his friend, Virgie, had died in Maui last month, O.D., he had taken to smoking Camels. She smoked Camels. She was only twenty-seven (compared to his ancient thirty-seven) and had been shooting up since she was fourteen. He met her when he lived in the Dharma Buddhist Center there.

Marlene came in to heat up some leftovers. She was wearing a fifties black slip and thirties vintage froufrou slippers with two-inch heels. She had on burgundy lipstick which carefully outlined her full mouth. She used a lip brush. Her hair was dyed "saffron" red and was mussed in that same kind of way that Marlene was mussed but sexy all over. Big calves. "Marlene," like her hair color, was not birth-given, but, like her hair color, her first and only theater director so far liked the name on her, so she made it hers. Last week her name had still been Eugenia. She was from Albuquerque.

Marlene helped herself to one of David's Camels and lit it on the stove. She turned to the closed door and made a face. The video that was playing in there was up full blast. Pointing with the thumb of the hand that held the Camel she whispered, "What's up?"

"OH NOTHING, NOTHING AT ALL!" David shouted. "IT'S JUST THAT *SOME* PEOPLE ARE VERY INCONSIDER-ATE, THAT'S ALL! THEY INVITE GUESTS OVER TO CRASH FOREVER, GIVE OUT THE APARTMENT KEYS LIKE THIS WERE SOME KIND OF HOTEL WITHOUT ASK-ING ANYONE WHO LIVES HERE IF WE MIND OR NOT AND THEN GET MAD IF YOU GET A LITTLE FRIENDLY WITH THEIR GUESTS! THAT'S ALL! IT'S A REGULAR SOAP OPERA AROUND HERE: '*LOS JOTOS TAMBIEN LLORAN*'—STAY TUNED, DEAR, EVER SEE A GROWN MAN CRY?"

Marlene put a hand on her hip and squinted an eye as she sucked on the cigarette. Meanwhile the rice from the Chinese carryout which was being reheated for the second time was burning. David looked at the iron pot and at Marlene. He got up and started stirring. He whispered furiously, "First, he brings this young guy without asking us if we mind him crashing here . . ."

"Who? Who brought what guy?" Marlene asked. David had taken over the stove, so she sat down. A plate with a few crumbs on it was nearby on the table. She examined it. Blew off the crumbs and placed it in front of her. Presently David poured the burnt rice on her plate and put a pair of chopsticks in front of her. She stared at the chopsticks. He went to the drawer by the sink and pulled out a tablespoon and brought it over to her.

He sat down at the table and began to shuffle his tarot deck again. As he talked, he shuffled, laid out a Celtic spread, got angry with the cards, and repeated the process. "Jorge—our roommate! Haven't you noticed he brought that young kid here a few nights ago and he hasn't left? He's crashing in the parlor!" David was whispering and as he whispered he moved close to Marlene's face. Marlene ate her supper, smoked the cigarette, and stared back at David's wide eyes without blinking. Marlene had great eyelashes.

"I've been working overtime every night this week," Marlene said. "I hate my job. I hate my manager, too. But what can I say? I gotta work." She picked out the burnt grains with her fingers.

"Well, about three nights ago, Jorge brought this young cute guy over, right? Now, I don't know what's going on. First of all, Jorge has never been with a man as far as I know, but if anyone ever wanted to, it's him, and then he brings over this cute little salvadoreño he just met, who started making eyes at me from the moment he walked in the door, and now he's—Jorge's—got him crashing in our parlor! They're in there right now, probably getting stoned . . ."

"Is that Humphrey Bogart?" Marlene asked.

David stared at her for a moment. They both listened to the dialogue coming from the video. Then he nodded and went on, "Anyway, I *know* that this is part of Jorge's plan to get rid of me—and you, too, by the way."

"Me? What'd I do?"

"You didn't do nothing, honey! It's not about that!" David was still whispering. "The other night the three of us went out to this very chic straight nightclub for a drink. Two other guys I know happened to come in, they saw me, us, and came over and sat down with us. I could tell that Jorge was digging it. I mean, he's so repressed, it's not even funny! I could tell he liked all these men together, but he wouldn't admit it. You know, he only just got here from his village in Mexico a few months ago . . . anyway, he turned to me and his little friend, Greg, who, by the way, all the while was feeling me up underneath the table, and Jorge says, 'Why don't you two get up and dance?'"

"What'd you say?"

"What? And get our asses run out of that joint? I said, 'Why don't *you* go over and ask one of those women over there to dance with you if you're so eager to see someone dance!' That's what I told him." And then David let out a loud heckle. He started to heckle louder and louder and as he did he got up and went next to the closed parlor door and heckled at it. "Can you imagine? *I* was supposed to get up and risk getting my ass kicked by some bouncer for trying to dance with a dude in a straight bar! And I do mean it was straight, honey!"

No one came out of the parlor and David went back to sit down. "So meanwhile, all this time, this Greg kid is coming on to me. So I'm sure now that Jorge is setting me up for some kind of gay drama here! I'll go to bed with his friend, who he wants but doesn't have the courage to admit it, and that will give him reason to hate me and the next thing you know, I'll be outta here . . ."

"Why you? Why not him? And why me? What do I have to do with all this?" Marlene stubbed her Camel out on the plate and lit another cigarette using David's Bic. "By the way? When did you start smoking?"

"Ever since my friend Virgie died in Maui, a friend of mine who still lives there called and told me. It was awful, awful. She was only twenty-seven . . ."

"My age," Marlene said.

"Well, why *you*? Because Jorge doesn't want any women

around here. He wants this place to reek of testosterone, dear, even if he can't admit he wants to be with a man."

"What are you saying? Jorge hates women?"

"I'm not saying anything, I'm just saying what I *think* is his motivation. I asked the cards. They told me I'm right about his friend Greg. Greg's gonna move in and then all this drama will happen and then I'll be looking for another place."

"So is this Greg gay? I mean, supposedly Jorge isn't, right?"

"I don't know, I don't know anymore," David said, picking up the tarot and unconsciously shuffling them again. "I'm too old for these games anymore, that's all I know. I asked the kid the other night what was up and he said he's got a girl-friend. But here he is coming on to me."

At that moment the kid came out of the parlor closing the door quietly behind him. He had a big smile and no shirt on. "Hi!" he said to both Marlene and David. "Hi," they both said, staring at him with blank faces. "Got a cigarette?" he asked David and helped himself to a Camel.

Marlene lit his cigarette with the Bic. "Thanks," he said, cupping his hand over hers as she lit his cigarette. "Hey," he said, blowing out the smoke, "haven't I seen you somewhere before?"

David slammed down his deck of cards and picked up the pack of cigarettes to get one out. He rolled his eyes at Marlene. Marlene licked the corner of her mouth a bit and with prac-ticed finesse she wiped the corners of her mouth to make sure her dark lipstick hadn't smeared while she was eating. She laughed a little laugh like she didn't believe Greg.

"No, really!" He laughed along like he didn't believe himself either. He pointed at her with the hand with the cigarette. "Don't you work at Maurice's? You're the hostess there, ain't you?"

"Yeah, I do! I got a big promotion last month," Marlene

said, "from waitress to hostess. Now I get a minimum hourly wage. And no tips. I was better off before."

"Yeah," Greg laughed. "I knew it! I knew you looked familiar," he smiled at her and looked her up and down. He looked at David up and down and smiled at him, too. "Well, I guess I'll go back to the video," he announced and went back to the parlor closing the door again behind him.

"It's getting kind of 'Apartment Zero-ish' around here, if you ask me," David said. Both he and Marlene were quiet, left with the feeling that they had just had safe sex.

"Wasn't that a foreign movie?" Marlene asked after a few minutes.

"No, it's Hollywood, pure Hollywood, honey . . ." David stubbed out his cigarette as he got up and went to the parlor.

◁ Being Indian,
a Candle Flame,
and So Many
Dying Stars

I left the parlor midway through the video about the Chamula Indian and his dying boy and told Eugenia and David, who were sitting in the kitchen having a shot of mezcal that David took from his Buddhist altar to calm their nerves since they had both just been kicked out of a bar down the street for no other reason than that the bartender didn't like their faces, "I can't watch anymore. Is there any mezcal left?"

They both shook their heads. There had only been a tiny bottle of it, the size you buy on airplanes but I don't know any airlines that carry mezcal. I was trying not to cry since I am supposed to be the brave one of the group although they don't know that or seem to think so. "It is moments like this, watching that story about the Chamulas, that I know that I am Indian," I said in my own language and not in this one that I am speaking to you now because if I don't, like the Chamulas, my story will be annihilated and not heard.

Eugenia looked up at me, flushed with the alcohol she had just had, and said, "What are you talking about? Have you ever taken a look at yourself in the mirror?" Eugenia is a bit disrespectful, which sometimes is a very good thing for her as a mixed-blood woman, a mestiza, to be irreverent. But I've noticed that she is not very discerning about her disrespect, which at that moment was directed at me. If I am not considered the bravest of the group, or the smartest, I am the oldest. And no one seems to want to take issue with that fact. At the very least, it isn't very nice to be ornery with one's elders.

I've decided that Eugenia is an anarchist. I drew this conclusion one night when she called herself a leftist and later announced that she was giving up her acting career (which consisted of one small but important part in a play) and was leaving the country however she could manage it and as soon as she could, to be an American exile. I didn't understand what that could possibly mean since a person had to have a country—which she claimed she did not have—in order to be in exile. Although she considered herself a leftist I mostly observed her to be frustrated with everything, including my hope, my revolutionary work, and my action. Therefore it came to my mind and rested comfortably in my private thoughts that she was an anarchist.

I liked her very much and I'm sure my age granted me saintly patience so I usually did not acknowledge her disrespect with words, but always made a gesture as if to slap her upside her head. But of course I never did.

"*Who* has ever told *you* that you are not Indian?" she asked in disbelief.

"Many people, believe it or not," I said.

"Like who?"

I wished I had been offered that bit of mezcal because I was still shivering from the video about the Chamula father traveling and traveling on foot with his feverish boy on his shoulders, looking for a doctor and, being an Indian, there would be no doctor, so I had stopped the video halfway, as I said, knowing also that Indians must walk even after death.

"Once in New Mexico I was going to a house blessing ceremony at the Zuñi pueblo and a white woman said to me: 'I don't think the Zuñi are allowing white people to attend this year.' 'I'm not white,' I said. 'To the Zuñi people you are as white as I am.' That's what she said to me. After a moment of recuperation, I said, 'It's true that my people are not Zuñi, but I'm not white.'"

"And it's not true that the Zuñi people would see us as white!" David said in a loud voice. Eugenia said nothing because she was angry at everybody. This little story had served only as one more brick on the wall she was building against a world of nations, to none of which she belonged.

There are things that I am. There are things that I am not. There are also some things that change. For instance, I was not always the oldest of a group. For a long time, I was always the youngest member and very quiet. I listened in order to become a person. Now, in such groups, I do most of the talking.

The young ones are not always listening, however.

"I know that," I said to David and looked at Eugenia, "but that is what she said to me. And in New Mexico, I had another woman, who identifies herself as *nuevomejicana*, also say that I am not Indian. So I asked her, 'Then what am I?' 'Hispanic, of course,' she said, *'we're* Hispanic.'"

Eugenia shook her head because she is from New Mexico and I think she felt ashamed.

Having made my point, which in this case was like being told to tie a double knot one more time, I went on, "When I was in Paris speaking at the Sorbonne I was asked by the students, 'Now that you're here, where do you feel you belong?'

"Come to think of it, I don't know what they meant by

that question, but what I understood is how I answered so I said, 'My spirit belongs to the Americas. I've been there for thousands of years. I'm sure of that now that I'm here.'"

Eugenia had nothing to say because she had never been to Paris but also because she did not know what to say.

David nodded. It was like that for dark people in Paris, he added. They went there to get away from not being wanted where they were born, except for the Algerians. The Algerians went there to work as well as to be not wanted there.

"Of course, in Paris, I was not considered an American, either," I said. "I stayed with a French woman who spoke nothing but French. She was a mathematician and was useless with language. So she invited her socialite sister so that she could come and converse with me. She was married to a doctor and they had lived in the United States for many years.

"The sister came over while I was in the kitchen helping with the dishes. She stuck her head in the kitchen. We exchanged glances. And then she said very loudly to her sister, 'So where is the American?' She had mistaken me for the maid."

"But she said it in English," David said. "Presumably her sister didn't understand English. So, for whose benefit did she ask that in English?"

"The American's," I said.

"So where did she think the American was?"

"I don't know," I said.

"People love to hate the United States," David said, "like a rich uncle."

"Yeah—rich Uncle Sam!" Eugenia said.

"And like that rich uncle," I said, "they tolerate it and are forced to cater to it, waiting and hoping for the moment he croaks to see if they were left in the will."

At that moment, Jorge came in. "How did you like the

video?" he asked me in our language, or rather, one of our languages. He had lent me the video. "It was beautiful," I said, "but it made me think too much of my son so I had to stop watching it."

"You have a son?" Jorge asked. Jorge and I really didn't know each other. "Yes," I said, of course, since I had just mentioned my son.

"Where is he?" he asked, as if at any moment my child would jump out from behind a half-opened door. The others looked uneasy, too. I don't know why. Maybe they weren't uneasy but the acknowledgment of an absent child was in itself an uneasy fact.

"He's with his father," I said.

Jorge nodded. He didn't ask anything more and I wasn't sure if this was because the question of the absent child was settled with the knowledge that he was with his father or because he didn't care.

There was some silence around the table. David lit the candle that was there and got up to turn off the kitchen light. This increased our solemnity. And with our solemnity our silence was given breadth. While I couldn't see it, I felt the moon over the desert, which were very far away, both desert and moon.

But I couldn't feel the stars, not the ones I slept under as a child. I couldn't feel their rapid oscillation as I always felt them in the desert, even when I didn't look out the door to verify that it was the stars making me tremble. The stars, like the moon in the city with high-rise buildings where these new and old friends had come together like family on the simple basis of sharing rent, were city stars. It was a city moon out there surely shining, although well hidden behind layers of smog and not giving any light to the world.

Then David broke the silence and staring without blinking at the candle flame he said, "I'm glad I'm not a father."

Jorge laughed nervously and lit a cigarette.

I stood up straight.

"Come on now, David," Eugenia said with a smile, "not all children are bad!"

"Children are people," he said. His eyes were transfixed on the flame and I began to stare at it too. "I'm not saying they are all good or all bad. They are people and they are not innocent simply because they are children."

Out in the city sky there were stars at that moment dying, the sun included. The earth was also said to be dying. And David, who my eyes and therefore my mind told me was across the table from me at that moment, was also dying at that very moment. We were all dying, of course, which is the nature of life. But David already knew about his death. His illness had a name but no cure. It had symptoms but no fixed cause. Each of us was helpless before it but David was helpless most of all.

So, out of compassion for David, who knew the name of his death and therefore all his thoughts were following after it, as if following a colon, I said, "Well, I am only responsible for the particular behavior of one child. And he is very self-assured, very loving, and very sweet."

Eugenia, out of a sudden sense of loyalty for something or someone, nodded but said nothing. Jorge didn't know my son so he nodded as one can only do to a proud mother who has just made such a comment. And David kept staring at the candle flame before it went out and left us in the dark.

◁ My Dream
Last Night

She slept in a tomb. She wrote that in her last letter. Mirna wrote to me faithfully. That's how I knew something was wrong. After that, no letter.

She had been through so much to be so young.

Our father took her, as the oldest, to that family to work for them. They said she would have a place to sleep and always enough to eat. She was about twelve at the time.

When I was fourteen I came to the United States with my godparents. They were investigating the chance of a new life here. I begged and begged my father to let me come; they were willing to pay like good godparents, and finally, yes, he said okay. But you have to bring her back, you know?

My father is not a bad man or a bad father, only too many children in his house and not enough food. Children go on the street to beg all the time. Not us. Our father took us to a rich family to work for them. First Mirna, then the next daughter, and I would have been next.

But instead I came here.

The man there, where Mirna went, began bothering Mirna.

She was too afraid to tell anyone. I don't blame her. No one would have believed her. She would have been punished. She kept working for the lady, who was a little nice anyway, but she, my sister, no longer wanted to sleep there. She slept on the floor, anyway, she said.

Many children go to the cemeteries at night to sleep, many women with their children. It is cool and clean inside a mausoleum. Marble floor sometimes. Very few bugs.

My father said she was found on the street, or that is, her body was found in the street, like rotten fruit, tossed there for the flies and rats. But I think it happened to her in the tomb. I think a man got her, a very much alive man.

I dream of her every night. She is sitting right outside the most beautiful white mausoleum in the country. It must've belonged to the president—the one that lived for too long and finally died, the only way he'd leave office. She is wearing that same little checkered dress she wore for years. The sleeves got too tight so she cut them off. "Too hot anyway," she said, smiling, taking a bite out of something. There are lots of palm trees. The sun is shining in her eyes. There is a warm breeze blowing her dress. She has rubber thongs on. Everything just like I remember her. I don't know. She looks happy, like she's posing for a picture. But she keeps telling me, "Remember to tell them about this tomb. Remember Mirna, my name is Mirna. Tell them I slept here."

How can I forget her?

But even though I am telling you, nobody listens.

◁ CHRISTMAS STORY OF
THE GOLDEN COCKROACH

We are on our way to see Paco and Rosa, who are getting ready to go home for the Christmas holidays, pack the four children, the assorted relatives who came to stay over the summer and never went back, the used clothes and appliances so treasured by those left behind in their Mexican village, load up the pickup-turned-camper with Paco's welding ingenuity, and head south on the three-day trip that leads to the tiny community in México by the sea where Paco and Rosa grew up, fell in love, and were married.

Their home in Norte America, the United States, is right in the middle of what now looks like the vestiges of a once-thriving area before the steel mills closed down and left the majority of its residents without means for a livelihood. Paco's extended family lives on the ground floor of the little brick house his father left him as legacy of the thirty-some-odd years he spent in Chicago working to support his family "back home." They don't use the storefront for much but to keep the junk Paco likes collecting and hanging on to for the time when he discovers what it will be good for. Right now there is a nativity scene in the window. Baby Jesus has not arrived yet. For twelve nights before Christmas the neighborhood children will come and sing Mary's pilgrimage songs. On Christmas Eve the statue of the Holy Infant will be carried in and placed on its bed of straw. The children love these evening meetings of prayer, song, and expectation, because afterward there are always special treats provided for them. Sometimes even a piñata, if a neighbor can afford it.

After the storefront area, you step right into a meager-sized kitchen with metal cabinets and a tiny table with a scratched laminated top, spotted black from a generation of service. To the left is a dark, claustrophobic room, floor covered with carpet scraps we gave them last year. That's Paco and Rosa's room. The crib for the latest baby is in there too.

Two steps up and you are confronted by two more rooms, equally dark and dismal. There are beds and mattresses scattered; none have blankets but are neatly made up with faded sheets. Since it's winter, I have a hope that the blankets are put away somewhere during the day the way beds are made sometimes where this family is from. I look around for a closet or bureau where such things must be kept but there isn't any.

There's an easy chair in the center of the room. Paco is relaxing on it this Saturday afternoon, the children clustered around him. It is then that you notice it for the first time on an old library table when you turn around to see what they're watching. It has a twenty-five-inch screen, or bigger if such a thing is made for the home, an ultramodern concave design with computerized mechanisms for color and volume control. It is so obviously in contrast to anything else in the entire room, entire apartment, entire neighborhood for that matter, that for a moment I just stand there watching Holmes beat Frazier in glorious living color before Rosa slips a lopsided chair with its guts spilled out under me and takes my baby from my arms.

It isn't long before the men have gone out to the garage where Serafín is going to build a wood-burning stove for Paco when he returns (in the middle of January!), when he will have to resume the modest body shop business he keeps his family going on until he finds a full-time job or when they just pack up and go home one day for good.

Rosa is fussing over baby. Her own children gather around, all cooing and staring with those huge, black eyes you see on paintings of little Mexican children—which is of course what they are, very perfect examples of them—Mexican children with tiny pouting mouths and full cheeks, just like my own baby.

Anyway, we have now moved away from watching the boxing match to the room where Rosa has placed baby on a small bed without a cover. This must be where her older sister sleeps. Cuca takes care of Rosa's children while Rosa goes out to doctors' appointments, conferences with teachers who want children to speak English at home too, offices that give coupons for milk if you qualify. Cuca is at the age where it is said she has been "left to dress the saints."

The children soon lose their interest in the new baby and are now playing trampoline on the twin-size mattress that's on the floor in the corner of the room. Did you apply for food stamps yet? Rosa asks. We can ask each other these questions because our husbands have both been out of work for a year, having met as prima donna welders at a nuclear power plant under construction that paid top dollar. A year of good wages did not make us all lose sight of our place in the spectrum of things or cause us to put on airs. Instead, we saved for such a time as this, and now even the savings won't get us through winter.

I tell her that Serafín went to the food stamp office but we were denied on the basis of having too much in assets. What did that mean? she wants to know. It means we have more than five hundred dollars invested in our three vehicles. But none of them run, Rosa says. I know, I say. The lady at the food stamp office suggested that Serafín junk them—then he could come back and discuss our eligibility for food stamps.

We talk about the children, their vaccinations, the cleft in baby's chin and who he may have inherited it from, and how Rosa would like not to come back in the dead of winter but Paco insists that the family stay together.

In the room with shadows caused by the dim light fading through the windows and a shadeless lamp on the floor, I reflect on the children fighting over whose turn it is to make somersaults on the trampoline/mattress and recall a room much like this one. Me, the smallest, getting pushed on the floor as big brother and big sister bullied their way to jump on Ma's bed when she wasn't looking.

It's during this distracted moment in the lapse between topics when something, like the flicker of a candle's flame, catches the corner of my eye.

I've been aware of the belligerence of the roaches in Paco and Rosa's house and how they don't worry a bit over the possibility of disgusting company with such abounding presence but go on with their business of keeping the order of their infinite world as they have since the beginning of time.

But what has caught my eye isn't a cockroach of the common strain; nor is this one of the lineage of winged grotesqueness that I've encountered when pulling the string to the light to the bathroom and am provoked to duck as if dodging bats. This isn't even the usual puny kind that makes its kingdom the kitchen cabinets, stove, bread box, and the shelves of the pantry.

This delicate example of verminous existence in modern civilization idling over the ripples of baby's blanket is shiny with a golden color no less brilliant than the wedding band I've worn since the day Serafín came home and presented it to me in a small velvet-covered box, on our first anniversary, just a week before my twenty-first birthday. That was during that ever-so-brief time of good fortune when he was at the power plant.

While I am inclined to brush it away and not smash it with the palm of my hand as I've felt compelled to do for a while in defense of my child's hygiene, but too stunned to do even that, Rosa's eyes follow mine until they, too, are on the golden cockroach.

"Paquito, bring me that jar," she tells the oldest of her brood, who stops his play immediately and runs off to the kitchen, returning in less than a second, or what might be half a mile traveled for the cockroach, which is by then determined to climb over the mountain that is my baby.

With the steadiness of a heart surgeon, using the tips of her fingernails, Rosa picks up the golden cockroach and closes down a lid with holes punched in it while the children and I have held our breath; she has done this without so much as bending one of the roach's antennae.

We are staring at the roach in the glass jar held up in Rosa's hand against the light of the shadeless lamp. The children's faces show ecstasy, and somehow I can tell no one but me is surprised that we are in the possession of what could be no less than a phenomenon.

"Give it some corn and for God's sake, don't drop that jar," she tells Paquito, who solemnly takes it from her hand and followed by the other children goes off to the kitchen.

"Rosa," I say.

"Yes?"

"That cockroach was gold colored."

"Not gold colored."

"Blond then."

"Not gold colored, nor blond. It *is* gold."

My expression must've become a complete blank because Rosa decides to honor me with a full explanation and assures me that she is also aware that golden cockroaches kept in jars and fed cobs of corn like mini-kings in some ancient, sacred ritual require an explanation.

"When Paco's father was a young man, already married with small children to support, but too poor and unskilled to do so, he went off to lose himself in the jungle where he spent an entire year." Rosa's story as told to her by her husband unfolds. "When he returned to his family he had with him a gold cockroach that he mated with a plain one in hopes of—"

"Reproducing golden cockroaches?" I interrupt.

Rosa shakes her head and corrects me. "In hopes of reproducing at least *one* gold cockroach. As it turned out, after much experimentation and tested patience, he discovered that one out of every twelve thousand eggs produces a cockroach of gold. Nevertheless, one time he had a pair of cockroaches. The life span of the cockroach is not very long, no matter how pampered it may have been. It took trial and error to find out what the most agreeable food for the cockroach was or at least its favorite, which is maize, as well as to be able to decipher the gender of a cockroach. Oh, my father-in-law had much to learn about the cockroach before he was able to have a gold male and female pair! He set out for the United States.

"Anyway, it was in this very house where he first found a room to rent. The store was occupied by the owner, who was an old Jewish pawnbroker. My father-in-law gave him one of his gold cockroaches, one of the twelve thousand offspring of the original pair no doubt, in payment for his room and board and soon found a job at the steel mill. The pawnbroker was very pleased with this kind of payment and always expected a gold cockroach on the first of each month from the young man who rented one of his rooms."

"What did the pawnbroker do with the cockroaches?" I ask.

"Melted them down. Although it required twelve thousand cockroach eggs to hatch before one gold one was produced, the landlord didn't mind that his property was being infested since it meant another gold one the following month. The house got so bad, the old pawnbroker's wife left him, as did the rest of the boarders. As much as he regretted it, he had to get out himself and join his family. He took quite a few gold cockroaches as payment for the house and left it to my father-in-law.

"He opened up another store, in another neighborhood, because soon every house on the street was infested with cockroaches, and since the gold ones are few and far between, and no one but he and my father-in-law knew they were actually gold and not gold colored, no one else benefited from them. My father-in-law continued to do business with him over the years. Whenever he needed money, he took the old pawnbroker a gold cockroach.

"When the steel mill closed down, my father-in-law went back to his village to retire with his wife and enjoy the many grandchildren they now have. He left the house to us since Paco also wanted to come here to work in the same trade."

"What do you do with the gold cockroaches?" I wondered out loud.

"This is only the third one we've found since we've been in this house. Do you suppose that the golden cockroach is becoming an extinct species? Anyway, the old pawnbroker still buys them from us."

"He's still alive?"

"Just barely," she sighed.

Serafín and Paco come in from the garage and Serafín gives me that look that husbands and wives give to one another when visiting that tells they are ready to leave and would prefer not to be protested. I wrap up the baby, slip on my coat, and we all make our way toward the kitchen, which we must pass through to get to the front entrance, which is at the junk-filled storefront.

In the kitchen the children are watching the cockroach-in-the-jar gorging on a half cob of corn. Rosa picks up the jar and shows it off to Paco, whose face lights up like a Christmas tree. A look is exchanged between them and she turns to me abruptly and hands me the jar.

"Here. Take it to the old man. I'll tell you where you can find him."

"But . . . what about you, the children, the trip back home?"

At that moment, Paco sweeps the jar out of my hand. "I have an even better idea," he says enthusiastically. Opening one of the cabinets and reaching in, he pulls out a cockroach and, lifting up the lid on the jar, throws it in.

"What? You don't want the cockroach to be lonely or what?" Rosa asks, confused by her husband's actions.

"It is possible that this pair may produce another one of gold, is it not?"

Rosa nods, catching on to her husband's idea. "But how do you know you have a matrimonial pair?"

After a moment of reflection on the now two-cockroaches-in-a-jar feasting on maize, Paco reaches into the cabinet again, running a hand over the surface, and pulls out another specimen for the jar. "And just in case," he says with a broad smile, one of satisfaction that he is able to do something for the family of another man in need, he casts yet one more potential mate for the gold cockroach.

I hand over the baby to Serafín and with the greatest care accept the jar of cockroaches from Paco, thanking them for their generosity and kindness as if I've just received one of those red sapphires that Imelda Marcos owns. Meanwhile, Serafín has no idea as to what's going on. I'll explain on the way home, I tell him and I do.

The cockroaches have lived in the jar on the maize for three days and so far I haven't noticed anything that seems like the beginnings of multitudinous reproduction. Maybe they need more room, or maybe they need privacy, Serafín suggests, and takes it upon himself to test out his theory by transferring cockroaches-with-corn to a shoebox, which he ties shut with a string.

Days later, we have cockroaches as tiny as lint specks climbing out of the slits Serafín cut through the top of the box to give them air. It isn't long before the predictable happens. The entire flat is infested with cockroaches, and we have not only not spotted another gold cockroach but have lost sight of the original.

We have to find the gold one, Serafín tells me desperately, with magnifying glass in hand scrutinizing the backs of all sizes and dimensions of cockroaches that now parade over every flat surface, latitudinal and longitudinal, of our home.

It is a week before Christmas and the tenants in the rest of the building are outraged over the recent infestation. They are sending bomb threats to the realty office that manages the building for the landlord, whose name we do not even have the benefit of knowing. Serafín and I keep Paco's father's secret as well as the old pawnbroker has for over thirty years. What would our neighbors do to us if they knew we were the cause of this new misery?

So we keep our cool the morning that the masked exterminators appear at our door and begin spraying something that smells like the equivalent of napalm on the world of vermin.

The next night I am still sweeping piles and piles of stiff-legged dead roaches. Serafín has given up the search among the rubble in hopes of finding a gold one. But a dead gold roach is probably as good as a live gold roach to the pawnbroker, rationalizes Serafín, who had no trouble accepting Paco's wild gold cockroach legacy. This must have had something to do with his having been looking for work for an entire year, the new baby, and the onset of what is predicted to be one of the worst winters yet, all accompanied by his eternal optimism.

We are watching one of television's countless news programs late one night when a golden flicker moving across the floor catches our eyes and almost at once we have both pounced on it. It is Serafín who comes up the victor, marveling at the gold creature as it languidly treads over his hand, down his wrist, and over the plaid flannel shirtsleeve.

"Don't lose it!" I gasp.

"Don't worry! Don't worry! I've got it. Where's the jar?"

We get the gold cockroach in the jar with the perforated lid and without another word we know what we're going to do with it. This one goes directly to the pawnbroker.

"He retired in Florida," someone tells us when we find the shop closed down without so much as a sign to direct us as to our next move. With the pawnbroker gone, we're stuck without the slightest notion as to where to take our gold cockroach.

"We'll wait until Paco and Rosa get back. They might have an idea," Serafín says.

That's not until mid-January.

So be it, Serafín sighs. We hop the 22 bus, the jar in a brown paper bag under his arm, me holding the baby.

◁ Mother's Wish

He is the most perfect child in the universe. She is the only mother. "If anything ever happened to you I'd kill myself," she whispers to him and punctuates her vow with a moist kiss on her baby's cheek.

In fact, nothing will happen to him, aside from the common childhood illnesses and his bouts of rebellion and brooding during adolescence and, finally, leaving her once he is grown. She won't have to kill herself. Instead, she'll take a ceramics class at the community college downtown. On Saturday nights she'll go to the Sundown Lounge and practice her two-step. Every Mother's Day, without fail, he'll call her from wherever it is that life finds him. She'll die happy. He won't ever die.

◁ THE LAW OF
PROBABILITIES

W here are you off to?" I asked her once. She pulled away softly, like hair through my fingers. She was like that pulling away, gone without my knowing it. "I'm off to meet myself," she answered. That was the kind of thing she said to me. I loved her so much.

Sometimes I cooked for her. She didn't care much for food, but she always thanked me and always ate what I prepared. I appreciated that, too, since I was never much of a cook.

Once our friend David was staying with us for a few days. She came home and said, "A freshman came to my office and said this to me: 'I have a crush on you. I can't help myself. I heard so much about you when I came to campus; that is why I took your class. Then I saw you on the first day, a gorgeous body and the face of a faded beauty . . .'"

And David burst out in a roar of laughter so that she couldn't finish. We both stared at him as he laughed louder and louder and rolled onto the floor. "I can't stand it," he said, finally, between laughter. "*You* . . . a 'faded beauty'! It conjures up scenes from *Sunset Boulelvard* and Gloria Swanson, the has-been silent screen star! We must take a picture of you wearing a turban!"

She stared at him, quietly amused that he was so thoroughly enjoying her story. After he stopped laughing she said, "No, I don't think so. Surely, people would mistake me for Lawrence of Arabia in a turban rather than Gloria Swanson." But he liked his joke better and didn't laugh.

I adored her sad eyes most. The rest of her face could radiate with joy or make you cower with its anger, but her eyes were always and forever sad.

That was because there was a part of her that was always and forever sad. It wasn't self-pity that caused this. The sadness never integrated with the rest of her. It remained a separate and constant element. Therefore, she could be well, pleasant, feeling kind; she could be passionate, bewildered by desire, torn asunder with anger; she could be anything, apathetic, uninterested, non-communicative, or nothing at all. But the sadness was always there, very much like the antifreeze used in a car and maintained at a certain level all year around to keep the car from overheating in summer and freezing in winter.

I don't want to go on about the sadness, but rather the eyes, which is where I saw it most. Once I snuck into the lecture hall where she held her weekly graduate seminar. I sat in the back but after a few moments she saw me. She smiled at me with her sad eyes. She was telling the students about herself. And while she was honest and forthright and did not hesitate to tell them about all her years in prison and that she did not regret killing her father, her voice was as soft as the coo of a pigeon. She may as well have been their grandmother telling each one a bedtime story while brushing her grandchild's hair. When she finished, I am certain they all resisted drawing close to her and putting their heads on her lap.

Surely there would be one who would go off to the dean afterward and demand to know why her parents were paying good money so that she would be instructed by a murderer, but that is probably why she told them about herself early on in the semester—to get rid of that one inevitable dissident.

When I first saw her I was a student, too. I was a senior and was not able to take any classes with her that year. I didn't have the courage to introduce myself until the following year when I returned to the university as a graduate fellow. I went to her office on the first week of classes. She was at her desk and I stood at the doorway for several minutes before she realized that there was someone else present. When she looked up at me, I blushed.

For a time, I tried to find out what other students thought of her but it was impossible to get a fixed opinion. It was as if there wasn't one her but many, ever changing, depending on the vision of the observer. Everyone thought they knew her. No one did.

I wondered if anyone saw what I saw when I looked at her. And again, opinions varied. The only aspect that was consistent with each solicited opinion was that nobody was indifferent. One might see her as that freshman fellow whom she told David and me about that afternoon, the "faded beauty," and the next would not say that her beauty was past but eternal and formidable like Coatlicue, the Aztec fertility goddess. Some, like David, thought it ridiculous to consider her age at all, since what intimidated those individuals was not her age but her authority, her undeniable volume of knowledge and, above all, her understated wisdom.

The men professors on campus did not ever understate their supposed savvy. They went around like pompous royalty flinging their invisible scepters and acting as if the entire student body should genuflect in their very presence. The women professors were few. They were scarcely visible. That is probably why they aroused so much interest among the students.

But she, alone, with her irrepressible sad eyes, and her expertise which was not refined like sugar but finely woven like silk, and her killing of her father at the age of sixteen, caused a mute uproar. The students did not flock to her. They did not crowd about her. It was obvious that she did not want that. One by one they came around, like that freshman did, like I did. They came, as if to pay homage, to place a symbolic flower before her and leave without being seen or heard.

She was given twenty-five years in prison but only did seven. When she was released she joined the Peace Corps. Then she studied and started teaching. This is how she told her story. It was never embellished and you could pull your hair out with exasperation that you had to ask point-blank direct questions to get the slightest detail about her story. "*Where* were you in prison? *Where* did you go in the Peace Corps? *Why* did you choose teaching?" Although she never said you shouldn't ask, the one forbidden question was: "*Why did you kill your father?*"

I, for one, had always been driven to great extremes of morbid curiosity regarding what her mother had thought of it all. She never mentioned her mother.

When I first went to her house on the hill, I noticed a black-and-white photograph of an older woman, "older" meaning hair gone white, wearing bifocals, in a porcelain frame. "Is that your mother?" I asked, trying to sound nonchalant, as if asking *her* about her mother in any context could be a question void of dark associations. "No," she said. I waited but she said nothing more. That was when I first realized that there would be questions that I would get answered and others that I would not, but that there would always be questions.

When she left me, it was at the end of the school year. It wasn't quite a year in the world's measure of time, but three seasons are quite a bit of time to spend with another human being. She did not say, "I'm leaving you." I don't know if that was because she was protecting me from the inevitable shock that the separation would cause or because she didn't know it herself at the time that she was leaving me. Instead she said, "I didn't get tenure." Since this announcement usually implied a form of death for an academic I knew I would experience a loss through whatever else she would say. "So what have you decided?" I asked.

"I don't know," she said. "I'll travel for a while."

"Will you write a book, do you think?" I asked.

She laughed, "If I didn't write it to get tenure, I sure won't write one now."

"But you could write a book for other reasons," I insisted. I, more than anyone at that time around her, knew that she could not write a book. One had to be convinced that there was merit in recording history since that was the purpose of writing, after all. It might be history that everyone agreed with or history that got you hanged for writing it but for which your name was revered in the future and then read to revise history. But it was all history and it was all myth, since history is myth. Starting with one's own story. More specifically, her story, which was a myth which she resisted to make into history.

One could only imagine what torment it must've been for her, whose very being was incompatible with the past, to go through school. I had never seen her degrees but she must have had them, otherwise how could she have gotten the post at the university? I was ashamed to have such doubts about her legitimacy but why was I having them at all?

I decided that my suspicion was due to a feeling of betrayal, but what had she done to betray me? And it went on like that indefinitely it seemed.

It felt like a long time before I heard from her again, but it was only months, which, of course, is a long time. Obviously, I did not expect for her to write so the postcard that came to me that day could have been from anybody but her. But I did hope it was from her. I didn't think it would be, but it was.

She was in Laos at the time that she sent it, but she was not in Laos anymore by the time I received it since one of the few things I could discern from her small, knotted handwriting was that she was leaving the next day, flying out to—?

I set the postcard, written badly and postmarked foreignly, faceup on the kitchen table. Occasionally I circled the table like a vulture in the desert wondering if that unexpected gift were dead yet. Later, before I went to bed, I held it in both hands, staring at the picture, then at the writing and back at the picture. I brought the postcard close to my face. There were no vibrations of dark sad faces, like hers, or like the multitude in the streets of Laos. There was no feeling of rivers or ocean. It had traveled across nothing to reach me but materialized through some futuristic space post office system. You write it, it's there. But did she write it? There wasn't even a signature. Off to the corner at the lower right-hand side was

with L
   o
  v
 e,

an illegible, signature.

When we were physically together, things were not like that, illegible, obscure, without return address.

When we were together, every Sunday morning I went out and brought back the Sunday paper and a white bag of croissants. She made coffee. We put everything on trays and went back to bed.

We made plans and carried them through.

We did not have a past, not her past, at least. She respected mine, if listening without judgment can be interpreted as respect. But she did not necessarily want my past, which did not matter. She did not want to give me hers either. That mattered to me, but not so much that I did not think we could create our own past moving forward together, together creating it, an aerial trapeze of two spiders with one web. I was very confused then—that she did not want this. I knew she did not want this, but she never said it.

Since then I was offered a tenure-track position before I finished my dissertation and have been offered the possibility of tenure once my dissertation/book gets accepted. I've had successful negotiations with a prestigious university press so I think I will most surely stay here.

My parents are very happy about this.

Last year I met someone. She's not in academia. One night I asked her, "Have you ever thought of going to Southeast Asia . . .?"

She laughed an uncomfortable laugh and asked, "Whatever for?"

"No reason," I answered. "I just wondered."

◁ A True Story

I had been watching her for a time. Not a young woman, as young women go, but a Creole woman's beauty manages to emanate exuberance as the years go on, like the bougainvillea in perennial bloom that, before you know it, has taken over the whole darn place. Her hair cascaded down to the narrow of her back, the blackness of it interrupted only occasionally by a silver strand here and there. She had the same yellowish-red hue to her skin as I do, which meant that mixed in with our slave ancestry, we had Indian blood in common. Or as some people would like to see it, mixed in with our French and Spanish ancestry there was a little Indian and African, too.

She kept her gaze fixed down on the latest edition of the *Picayune*, sipped her coffee with a certain finesse, picked up her beignet but never brought it up to her mouth, and along with other such almost imperceptible, nervous gestures I observed her to be somewhat lost—a quality which I have never been able to resist in a woman. Although she didn't ask, I brought her another glass of water. "It certainly is a

humid day!" I said, being more gentleman than any kind of
a waiter, I am sure.

"Yes," she said. "Yes, it is."

I stood at attention, although she didn't notice. Hearing
that voice, more melodic than a church choir, something like
the river on a June night, my knees unlocked. It was the only
time in my life that that actually happened to me.

◁ María Who Paints and Who Bore José Two Children

For a Marxist-Leninist-moderately-Maoist who'd spent his entire adult life with unflinching certainty that a revolution was not only necessary but inevitable, perhaps becoming a self-styled survivalist when the revolution didn't happen and heading for the hills of the Northwest was the next best thing.

What hills were they that her ex-husband was heading for with their children, María wondered from a city flat as the palm of her hand. She could have been seen standing at that moment at her window clear across from China were it not for the high-rises that skirted and laced the city like Portuguese needlepoint.

"Listen," said her ex-husband, who did not speak with the grace of Portuguese needlepoint but whose words instead struck her fast, always catching her off guard with the deadly intent of a flyswatter, "I don't know if it's gonna happen, or rather, I don't know exactly when, but I don't plan on hanging around waiting for it." José was calling from a pay phone, off a highway. She didn't know which highway. He didn't say.

The only thing María was certain of was that José had her children. Somehow, María thought, this was not what the courts had in mind when they granted her ex-husband the right to take the children for summer vacation.

She hadn't known it until then—until the call—but for over a year, José said he had been in touch with some very informed individuals he called survivalists. (No, not a religious sect, María, he wasn't that stupid, they're just people, like you and me, who have been following things, world events. They have maps.) They communicated with each other on the Internet. As in the Book of Revelation, the predictions of an apocalypse were manifesting themselves at the end of the millennium, one right after the next, the survivalists indicated, as sure as the eventual decay of a root-rotted tree. And they all agreed, the holy oak was on its way down.

To think she had been the one who'd taught him computer savvy. All she'd had in mind was that maybe it would help him get a clean desk job—get him off the highway, the one he had been driving on for twenty years as a trucker.

It was 2 A.M. when he hung up on her—with a slam, leaving a buzzing in her ear. She was trembling, slightly, not a lot, just enough to make her take out the bottle of brandy in the kitchen cabinet and pour a bit into a juice glass.

"All you do is criticize me! How come you never bring up all that I did for you!" José had screamed at her. "For ten years I hauled ass to support you and your work—to help make your artist dreams come true! Not to mention the support from my folks that you got—while we lived practically rent free and you got a free studio for ten years! And now that I want my son and my daughter to see that they are part of my family—this family that I have formed now—in the little bit of time I am allowed to have them, all you can do is pass judgment on me!"

Yes, he had hauled ass, as he put it, for her. He had been a good husband. She had not been in love with him and maybe, because of that, he was right to feel she had used him.

But in turn for José being a good husband, María thought, she had been a good wife. She cleaned house, did laundry, cooked all the meals, cared for the babies without asking for his help. And if she had not been in love with him, he had not been in love with her either.

She never thought about love. When she thought about beauty she thought about painting. She painted hard and long and every spare minute between housework and children's needs. He spent days and nights away on the road. She felt she was doing her share and he did his.

When he came home after a week on the road, she cooked for him. She cooked chicken, because that was his favorite, and in winter, lots of soup. He really liked her soups. She saw that he had fresh underwear, pressed pants. But yes, it was true, she had not ever been in love with him.

Until María fell in love she had not known that she wasn't in love with José. She didn't plan it that way—falling in love with someone else. She didn't even want it. But there it was. Right after she told José, he went out and got himself another woman. Right after. If María had not been in love with her husband, he also was not in love with her. Although José never admitted it, now she knew that, but the point for José was not that he had never been in love with María either. He had hauled ass for her and she had left him for someone else and that was the summation of their marriage.

It was around then that she met Karl Weber, a German artist living in New York. He saw her paintings at a street fair that summer. He was sure of her paintings. He talked her into sending slides to his agent. One, two, three—each step was small, measured but certain. A decade later, María is selling her paintings at top dollar and she is Karl Weber's protégé and lover.

He still keeps his studio in New York and she has held down the fort in Chicago where she has lived all her life. Where José has lived since the age of two when his family moved there from Corpus. For both María and José who speak a lot of Spanish but mostly English, Chicago cold and hot is home. Chicago racist and resplendent is home. Chicago is holy and evil. It is home for María, home for her children. It is home for their grandparents, aunts, cousins.

It is where she paints. She has painted very large paintings and very small ones. Some she has thrown away before dawn. Some hang on strangers' walls now. One or two have won prizes.

Where is José off to?

María never thought of herself as beautiful, sexy maybe, before the kids, she had thought,but not glossy-page rosy-lipped Isabella Rossellini smashing. But one day she found out that she was beautiful. She was beautiful for the first time at the age of thirty-two, breathlessly, drop-dead-diva beauty transformed by her woman lover whom María had loved complexly, somewhat confusedly, at times utterly confidently, but always with urgency—which was why she left José without so much as a note.

But things changed quickly. Phyllis, the lover, pleaded, "Tell me you love me! Tell me you're never gonna walk out on me!" Promise me this, pledge me that. And meanwhile, María sat in her now rented studio (since José's parents had evicted her as soon as they heard of her infidelity and perversion), staring at her paintings, tiny and big, and wondering if she would ever in her life produce one piece worth the canvas it was painted on.

Phyllis and José having it out every time José came by for the kids on the weekends.

María painting.

José's new girlfriend telling everyone in town that José's wife is a lesbian. Poor José!

María's sister, having heard the word on the chismografía line and crying in María's kitchen: "Please María, go see Father Vincent. Talk to him. He'll help you see your way clear— think of the kids . . . Think of how this will affect Ma if she knew!"

Everyone focused on María the Irresponsible. She left her kids' hard-working father. She chose art. As far as anyone knew she wasn't even a real artist. María all over town with a dyke. They actually had the children with them. Where's José? Poor man! Some wanted him to come up with the child support to help María get out of that basement flat where she'd gone to live with the kids. Others thought he should take the kids out of that unhealthy environment—and they were not referring to the basement only.

Years went by.

Phyllis long gone.

Karl Weber finally told her he loved her last year at her opening in New York.

"Now you're moving to New York! Everything's okay to do as long as it benefits your career!" José screamed at her. The other side of his long silence was this: ten years of pent-up rage and frustration, at this moment directed at her. "Well, this is something *I* have to do! I don't know for sure if there will be a world crisis, but if it comes, I want to be ready. The banks will all go broke; there'll be chaos in all the cities. California will fall into the ocean! It's all predicted. It's not me saying this, there are people out there, they study these things. There's a lot more about this that I can't get into right now, but—" And for an instant perhaps José forgot his hatred for the mother of his children and remembered that she too was part of that large mass of helpless humanity he felt for, so after a brief pause he added, "You should think very seriously of finding refuge out in the country somewhere, too, for when the time comes . . ."

"And if California doesn't fall into the ocean soon and if the banks don't all go broke and nothing happens in the cities?" María asked. "If Moses doesn't have to lead his people through the desert to safety? Let's just say, for instance, that he couldn't part the Red Sea?"

"Then, well, we will all look at this as an adventure," José replied.

"Send my children back home at the next airport," María ordered. María who orders. María who is selfish, who takes and does not give. María who only thinks of her career. María who after she made it big never thought to pay back her in-laws a dime for all those years of free studio space. Isn't that so, María, isn't that so? María for whom he hauled ass only to be dumped, cuckolded by a pair of dykes. Did it matter that it had been a woman? She didn't know. María who is now with a rich European fat cat—an egotist artist just like her. Just what she always wanted. This is how José saw her. Never María who loves her babies more than anything in the world—María who wanted each pregnancy even while José shook his head each time at the news. Not María who has lived for ten years providing for their children, taking them to school, to music classes, on trips. María who reads to the children every night. María whose babies are now honor students. María who would throw herself in front of her children to stop a bullet, who'd wanted to have babies so as to give them all the love, all the pretty things she never had, protect them forever—and who found out from the moment of their births, because she'd heard their screams when taking the first breath of life, she would never be able to protect them from all the pain the world doles out to each human being, that there would be a bullet she'd never see coming. María who scans her memory for a dream, a very bad dream, a foretelling of doom so that she can see what José sees, so that in a strange way she'll be less afraid and believe what he believes, doesn't find one, can't find one—but for the one reverberating question: where are her children? "Where are my children, José?" Her fingers are cold and sweaty as she grips the phone, pressed close to her ear.

"Go to hell, María," José hangs up.

José is on a highway. María doesn't know where. The children are sleeping in the back seat of his van. They are with Daddy. They are going on an adventure.

◁ CRAWFISH LOVE

She was my waitress each time I went into Mares Mazatlan but I did not notice her until the third time I was there. They say the third one's the charm or something like that. Anyway, because everyone that worked there wore name tags, I knew her name right away: Catalina. I did not have a name tag—customers obviously are not obliged to wear name tags, and I'm not really accustomed to going around with one on myself, except at regional meetings where we're always required to stick a name tag on, you know? You forget and go around all over town, the gas station attendant and any jerk on the street saying, "Hello, Vanessa!" Meanwhile, you · keep wondering what the hell's going on—are these guys psychic or something? Then, when you get home your kid brother tells you, "You can take off the name tag now, stupid." Then you yourself go, "¡Tonta!," and give yourself a slap on the forehead.

Catalina with the name tag and the ruby red mouth only stared at me kind of funny that day when I said, "Hey, Catalina, what's up?"

She wore her hair real big which was the way younger girls were wearing it at that time, girls in high school, I mean, and girls who were unemployed moms, girls who worked as waitresses. I was a professional so I couldn't go around looking like that anymore. Actually I was in training but at the end of a three-month period, I would be an official salesperson at Fuji International Computerware, a huge international company that had just opened up a little branch in our town the year before. I had taken a few computer classes at the tech school while looking for something besides waitressing and cashiering at the local discount stores and I was happy to be alive the day after I put in an application and I got the call that they were interested in checking me out. I felt a little bad for my dad who also went with me to apply, because he had been unemployed for a year and there was no hope of him getting his job back since that company had closed down and moved to Mexico.

Mares Mazatlan was a new restaurant, featuring as its specialty crawfish enchiladas. Beaumont is one of the few places, I hear, where you can even get crawfish enchiladas. My girlfriend from Fuji, Eliana, and I, being the only two Mexicans in the training program, went with our supervisor and two of our co-trainees to check it out. We kind of considered ourselves the experts on Mexican food at Fuji and when we got to Mares Mazatlan we acted like the entire patronage from Fuji depended on our report. Well, this is not at all a story about food so I'll just tell you that (just like I've tried to tell Catalina a hundred times but she still doesn't believe me) although I noticed her the first time I was there I was too wrapped up with trying to impress my colleagues to separate Catalina from her job. And if the truth be known, I only said "Hey, Catalina, what's up?" to show off in front of them, as if saying hi to the Mexican waitress was something only another

Mexican could do. But I liked how waitress-like she conducted herself, filling up our water glasses every five minutes, making sure we did not touch the plates that had obviously been placed on volcanic rock to keep our enchiladas hot: "¡No tocan los platos! ¡Están calientes!" she yelled at us, and me and Eliana quickly jumped at the opportunity to translate like we were at the United Nations or something. "A fine little waitress" my supervisor from Fuji said when we were dividing up the check. "Yes, a fine little waitress, a fine little restaurant," Eliana echoed and in her way, overdid it just enough, as usual. Eliana was very eager to make a career at Fuji.

I'm ashamed to admit it but on that first official visit I, too, thought of Catalina only as a fine little waitress. Actually, she's not that little, and I'm also ashamed to say I didn't notice that either at first. Ambition will do that to you, blind you, leave you like an eyeless crawfish to drag your little, shelly self around without realizing what a pathetic creature you are and meanwhile, what? To end the metaphor? We all end up in the same boiling pot in the end.

Nor the second time did I notice Catalina. The second time I actually tried the crawfish enchiladas. Well, I know I said I wouldn't talk about food here but they were pretty good. That's why I decided to go back the following week. This time I did not go with my co-workers who did tend to distract me to no end enough at work, what with all the competition to see which twenty of the forty-two trainees Fuji was going to keep. I was getting worried that, unlike Eliana who worked at perkiness despite her imperfect English, I just didn't have enough personality to be seen as computer sales finalist material for Fuji.

I went to Mares Mazatlan to drown my sorrows in some crawfish posole, which was their newest specialty.

"What's up, Catalina?" I said, less enthusiastically than

when I was with the Fuji crowd. But, as I mentioned earlier, she hardly looked at me anyway, part of the mass blur that made up the luncheon rush, I suppose, and didn't even bother to respond. She came back a minute later and took my order, again without making eye contact. Without even looking once at me. Meanwhile between Catalina pouring water into a plastic tumbler she plopped in front of me, wiping the table with a rag, and snatching the menu before I finished saying, "Special, plea—," I found myself feeling something that I had not felt before. I shielded my face with my hand, hoping she wouldn't see me blushing. What I was suddenly feeling was something like discovering you still have your name tag on on the street, but worse, more like a combination of the name tag, a piece of toilet paper stuck to your shoe when you've come out of a public restroom, plus, maybe, discovering afterward that you had a little spinach lodged between your front teeth at that precise moment when you mustered up the courage to say hi to someone you've had a crush on for a month. I said hi again from behind my hand.

I checked my shoes under the table which were okay, noticing Catalina's size sixes while I was looking down there. I can always tell exactly the size a woman wears. I'm giving myself away more than I care to now, but what the hell, which is what I said to Catalina after she let the bowl of crawfish posole hit the table with a *pas*! so that a few drops of red chile splattered on my only silk blouse. Catalina stared at me but did not apologize. "Catalina," I asked, "you like to play pool?"

◁A LIFETIME

He is tubes all over. He is also bald. I think he had been losing most of his hair already anyway, but now his entire body is hairless.

The last time I saw him we rendezvoused in secret downtown at Christmastime. Even though he was afraid that his wife would question him, he bought me perfume on his credit card.

That was five years ago.

Our life together was a lifetime ago.

Since then, he has been married for nearly twenty years. Nearly twenty years, is what his wife must tell everyone, when she shows off pictures of their children, a boy and a girl, when she talks about their home with the new deck he built last summer, when she recalls their honeymoon every anniversary.

But it isn't twenty years because twenty years ago is when we got married. We had no honeymoon.

He doesn't recognize me at first when I come in. I've intentionally gone to the hospital in the afternoon when I believe she may be at work. She is very dedicated to her job. He says she likes money. But she also liked the idea of a life devoted to a family, a husband, a boy and a girl, a house with a new deck, a brand-new fully equipped recreation vehicle. They take trips to Disneyworld every summer.

I never thought he'd go for that, at least not when we were married. I thought he didn't like kids. I didn't want to have any then, either, so I just figured neither did he. He was a musician.

He became a contractor. He never had much of a mind for business so he has always worked for someone else.

He doesn't recognize me right away, too groggy from medication. He thinks I'm a nurse.

We thought we were all grown when we married. I had been out of high school for two whole years. During our one-year marriage, neither of us held down a job. We had no real skills. I was always a lousy typist. He wanted to get into the union but in those days, they didn't let Puerto Ricans in unions.

I tried to find out something from the nurse in charge, about the tumor. She said I'd have to talk to his doctor if I wasn't part of the immediate family.

When we got married I was pregnant. We knew we weren't ready for a family. We didn't want to throw ourselves into a factory all our lives as our parents had done.

I've never had a family.

He smiles when he finally recognizes me, but I know he is nervous that his wife will walk in. She has never allowed him to talk about his marriage to me, not to her, not to their friends and family. I was erased from his history. I saw them together in a restaurant once. He looked so upset, I went right by them to my table. He would have introduced us, but what was the point?

He said I was not the marrying type. Each time I get married he says that.

I put the bunch of irises in a plastic container used for collecting urine. Of course, it's clean and I've put water in it. He takes the little notecard, reads it, and slips it under his pillow.

"So how's your career going?" he asks. He is twenty-one years old again. He is cute and charming. He is not middle-aged, tired, and very likely not going to leave this hospital alive.

I nod. I shrug my shoulders. I am pretty. I have the best pair of breasts on anyone we know. I am going to take the world by storm. I am not overweight, wearing bifocals, and looking for a new job.

He puts his hand out and I take it. We both look to the door reflexively. "You look great," he says. I think he means it. He probably means it because I am not the one in the hospital bed dying.

"So do you," I say.

We spend an hour like that, holding hands, me sitting on the edge of his bed, he dozing off, wondering what day it is and if the staff will relent and let his kids come up to see him later.

◁ Conversations with an Absent Lover on a Beachless Afternoon

◁ 1

I can assure you that the last thing I want to do is to scare you off, away, further than you are headed already because you are, in your own words, just starting out your life, and I, by my own account, am halfway done. It is not my intention to stop you. No one stopped me, try as he—or she—might. I kept moving, like a shark, in one concentrated direction. No, never has anyone stopped me. Nor can anything, short of death.

◁ 2

When I was seven years old, my papi and the boys left on a two-week vacation to Mexico. He didn't have a steady job. No matter, Mami did. She, being a good Mexican woman, did not try to stop him. She kept working, said nothing to the neighbors. I, taking her lead, did not utter a word of his absence to anyone either. Two weeks passed. The boys had rented a ten-room villa in Cuernavaca. They were living the high life.

Late-night collect phone calls until my mother wouldn't accept anymore. She couldn't afford them, she told him. Six months passed. Papi showed up early one morning, just before Mami left for work. It was still dark. After the high life, the maid, the gardener and his family, the chauffeur, the parties with Hollywood stars, Elizabeth Taylor (sans Eddie Fisher, or was it Richard by then?), the tailor-made sharkskin suits, he came back without so much as the suitcase he left with. Al, the leader of the boys, stayed behind to do five years in a Mexican prison, taking the rap for the marijuana trafficking that had kept them in that nouveau riche lifestyle. Papi woke me up, who by then had become Mami's bedmate and was in her/their bed lost in my sleep. Papi. A big hug. He brought me a small seashell on a keychain, painted with a tiny palm tree and on which was written *Cuernavaca*.

◁ **3**

You first came to my apartment some four or five weeks ago, and it was all electricity and vanquishing loneliness and cigarettes and did I also have a beer with you? You had come to talk to the writer and ended up staying the weekend. When you left on Sunday night, you preferred to walk back home, left your motorcycle in the parking lot, needed to leave something behind, you said, proof that it had all really happened.

◁ **4**

Papi and the boys went out every Friday and Saturday night. They liked to go to the jazz clubs, to the Rego Theatre, to the Aragon Ballroom. They heard Charlie "Bird" Parker, Stan Getz, Cal Tjader on the xylophone, Willie Bobo, Mongo Santamaria blinding fast on the congas. They dressed in their best suits, rode up in Cadillacs, gave big tips to the parking valets. Cadillac Cat (arino) was the mechanic of the crowd and he kept all their rides running smoothly without charge, or just a few bucks if you had it on you.

We lived in a flat on the second floor in the back of a—not to be cliché but simply frank here—rat- and roach-infested building. It was a little scary coming home after dark because the bums and cutthroats hid under the stairs leading up to our porch, shooting up, pissing, drinking whiskey.

After the show, the boys went down to Chinatown to Lucky's, an all-night Cantonese joint where Papi always ordered the same thing: beef egg foo young. When I moved to California, moons and decades later, and he came to visit, he said there were no good Chinese restaurants in California because none we tried served egg foo young. Or at least, none served anything like what he was used to at Lucky's.

Mami liked Chinese food, too. So, at about two or three in the morning, whenever Papi got home, he'd wake her up. With him, he'd have those little white boxes packed with cold hard white rice and, in another, Chinese greens, because greens were Mami's favorite. She was never finicky about food, being poor all her life made her that way. Before she got diabetes, she'd try anything. Years later, without flinching an eye, she ate the escargot I brought home from a date once. She said she had even tried frog legs somewhere. When she watched a TV show, and there was a dinner scene, Mami lost interest in the dialogue, trying to figure out what it was they were eating, each time saying aloud how much she'd like to have a little taste of whatever it was they were enjoying so much.

◁ 5

"Here's the thing," I start to say to you, this morning. My head is pounding and you have been taking off, leaving to start your life, to end your days as a student and become (a terrifying thought to you) a responsible member of society, of your family, be a good son, go back home.

I am not a college sophomore. It means nothing to me if you can make no promises when you leave. I am worried about today, the work I have to do, writing I must nearly slit wrists to get to.

"So, what's the 'thing'?" You jab at me, like a jock on a basketball court. I can see it is true what all the faculty on campus fear about partying, even once, with students. They lose all respect for you afterward. "See?" you say. "You don't even know what the thing you are talking about is."

I stare at you, still groping for the "thing" that I know. Only how do I tell it to you?

◁ 6

His birthday is tomorrow, but twenty-two years ago, on that day, Mami busted him with his girlfriend. A beautiful Polish girl who was twenty-four years old at the time. Papi was turning thirty-five. Mami had bought him a couple of cool sport shirts as a present. She also brought him a new set of timbales. Because our landlord did not let us play music in the flat, Papi said he had taken them over to Al's house. Papi had been out all night, said he had gotten pretty loaded and was picked up by the cops coming home and thrown in the drunk tank.

Once he went to sleep, Mami, who had taken to searching his pockets, found a cleaner's ticket. There was our last name on it but with an address that was not our address.

Even though we left Papi sleeping, by the time we got to that address—which was three bus rides away, in the white section of town—his Caddy was parked right in front.

We stared at each other when we got up to the door, then Mami pushed it open, without knocking. There he was, dressed in one of his new swinging birthday shirts, and as always, whenever out in the world, although he was inside, he was wearing his shades.

Annette—because she had a name now, it was Annette, and very suitable too, I thought—was petite and had her hair frosted. She was sitting on the couch across from Papi, who sat, cross-legged on a La-Z-Boy chair, in a way that made you know right away that it was his chair, his place in that room. They had not so much as stirred when Mami and I burst in.

They had had a big row the night before, Annette began to babble. (Introductions were not needed.) She was trying to break up with Papi because he would not leave his wife. He had forced his way into her house. His arms were covered with fingernail scratches. She had called the cops. I had never heard Papi so much as raise his voice at home.

Mami, who up until then had never been any good with English, did a good job getting her point across then and there. "So!" she started, sweeping across the room. (Papi and Annette frozen in their places.) "Here are the timbales I bought you for your birthday!" And *pas*! The timbales went flying in a loud way, the LPs, too, that Mami knew were his, Pérez Prado, Machito, Ray Barretto, his man.

"Just tell me one thing, Nat," Annette said from where she sat on the couch. "Do you love me?"

Mami stopped flailing things about and looked at him. I stopped crying long enough to look at him, too. He was just too cool. Then, expressionless—you couldn't see his eyes behind those dark glasses—he said, "Yeah, of course I love you, Annette."

◁ **7**

"Is it the truth that you wouldn't come to speak at our class because the professor couldn't pay you?" you asked me last night when you dropped by. "You wouldn't lie to me, would you? Otherwise nothing we have said to each other means anything. I mean, the professor said that about you, but I knew better. I figured he was lying—to boost himself up or to make us think you are that way. Did he even ask you to come?

"I know that he can't stand the fact that you are in demand everywhere and that he's not anymore. The sad part of it is, is that *I* have read his stuff, and the man used to be bad [bad meaning really good here] and it's too bad he has to act that way now toward younger, up-and-coming writers. But have some pity on him, will you? One day, a younger writer is going to come up behind you, too, and you will know how it feels . . ."

"*That* will never happen," I tell you. I am, after all, a writer, not a dancer. If I know anything, am sure of one blessed fact about this life I lead, it is that. *I* will never depend on my past glories. *My* work just gets better. *I* get better, and I am going to keep it up until I drop dead with pen in hand.

◁ **8**

You understand. You have this arrogance too. Otherwise, why would you ever have showed up at my door, late one Friday night, with a six-pack?

◁ **9**

"He was very proud of you," Ash Can told me at the wake. Ash Can, who, more than Papi, could never hold down a job. Mexico, dope, music, women, all the same stuff.

"And I, of him," I answered.

◁ **10**

I have this friend who is a writer. She says her lovers hate the fact that she fictionalizes everything that happens between them. Even in the throes of a heated argument, she will stop to take notes, telling herself, remember how he looked when he said this, what you were wearing and exactly how it felt to say such and such. And they hate it, her lovers. She writes pretty tight stories, too. She doesn't give a hill of beans what they feel about it. There are always more lovers. There are always more stories to write.

Papi did not like the book I wrote about him. I knew this because he said nothing about it. But when he came to see me in California, after he'd had a few beers, I readied myself. "I feel like my life is an open book," he said. (Just like Nat, never one to pass up a cliché.) But, having anticipated that I'd need a reply since the family boycott of my book, I shot back, "It isn't your life, it is my life. And it isn't your book. It's mine."

◁ 11

"So, you're going off to live your life, that's okay," I tell you this morning. "You will go back home to your family, get a job, hopefully, and pay back your school loans, travel some time, maybe . . ."

"Hey! This is *my* life we're talking about here," you protest, resenting the underlying lack of enthusiasm I have, my obviously bad attitude (bad not meaning good here). "You say I am going to travel in the same tone of voice as paying back my loans. Traveling is *supposed* to be exciting."

"Yes, you will have a good time traveling. You will meet your pseudo-innocent twenty-year-olds to enjoy without commitments, sit in an open-air cafe drinking a beer with your brother whom you have brought along to share adventures, and at a given moment, when least aware that you are even thinking of this, you will say to yourself, '*She* is somewhere right this minute probably sitting in an open-air cafe, also getting drunk.' And what you are doing at that moment will suddenly feel no different than working and paying off your loans because *I* won't be with you and you'll be wondering where I am."

"And with *whom*," you add, looking away, just as you always do when you can't look into these eyes embedded with too many memories that don't include you.

▽ **12**

"There's something to be said about innocence," you said to me last weekend, when I snatched you away on a rendez-vous, to meet my friends in San Francisco, to see theater and Almodovar's latest film, to drink at a Latino cross-dresser bar. You said this with regards to the twenty-year-old sophomore you had sent on her way (not without some reservation), so that you could spend more time with me. You struggled for three weeks with how to tell her because you so much did not want to hurt her feelings. Innocence was something that she could give you and that I could not, you told me. Innocence in females to feed the male lover's ego held its place in nine-teenth-century romance novels. Also, always in Mexican soci-ety—which you, she, and I share.

Was I to serve my life as the perennial apprentice of a man, be a static symbol of innocence—which men yearn to believe in, in this havoc of a world they've created? Is that what you expected from her?

Once innocence—an all-too-brief state of being, if such a one exists—encounters experience, it is transformed. If that transformation is understood, it becomes knowledge. And if that knowledge is employed, then it has become wisdom.

I so much prefer the wisdom in your eyes to the innocence of your remarks.

◁ **13**

I have another friend. She turned fifty last month. Like you, me, the twenty-year-old sophomore, she has lived her life at the outposts of Mexican culture here in the United States. She is in love. He is twenty years her junior and wants a family. His mother, who has never met my friend but only spoken with her on the telephone, is happy for them and wants grandchildren from her only child, her son. She does not know my friend's age.

All this notwithstanding, my friend is in love. She wakes each morning, dreaming of having a child. She wants the status that comes with being a mother; everything else she has worked for thus far, everything she has accomplished is practically without meaning, compared to motherhood. Do you think a woman can be innocent at fifty? A woman without a child remains a child, a being that is more man than woman but really neither? Or does simply being loved by a man make her lose her innocence?

◁ **14**

Mami had two children when Papi met her. Was Papi looking for innocence in Annette? There was the same age difference between them as there is between us.

The facialist examined me up close the other day. Being Californian, she felt compelled to read my "aura" before applying steam, then clay masks. "At first, I thought that your eyes held lots and lots of sadness," she said.

"But no," she reconsiders, after an hour of talking and doing things to bring color back to my skin. Far from pale, I am Earth-dark like you. But all this holding in of sadness and all this suspended time, waiting to finish up here, have caused my skin to turn sallow. "No," she says, "those are survivor's

eyes, the wise eyes of the poet that you are. Be good to yourself.
Find someone who will make you laugh. You only need to
bring back that glow your inner being radiates. Poets do very
important work. They come here to heal the planet, but they
must protect themselves. They feel everything."

◁ 15

"You are so wise, m'amor," I say to you last night. You
think I am making fun of you. Who has ever called you wise?

When I am certain that one more layer peeled away will
cause me to die from overexposure to this life, it is my child,
who is not quite seven, who teaches me how to keep opening
myself.

You are wise because you know how to laugh. And you
make me laugh with you.

"You will have to record my memoirs," I say, not laughing,
but maybe not seriously either. "You will know how to keep
the humor in how I saw things."

"Maybe that's what I've come to do," you say, you who,
unlike me who must learn from a child, are always open to
possibilities. You never deny me any request, at least not with
words.

"No, you are destined to live your very own life, and among
the things you might choose to do along the way, is to remember me."

You don't have to write it down. Just remember me.

◁ 16

"So the 'thing' is this," I announce after we have had coffee
in the morning and you are ready to leave, to have your day,
doing who knows what or where. While I feel that dragon
called what I do breathing fire inside me and will spend my
day inside, alone, writing. I have found the thing and I must

let it out. I want to give it to you, have you take it with you, carry it in your shirt pocket, if not somewhere in your entrails: "I am not polished. I am not whipped cream. I do it raw," I say, and immediately you stop at the door. I can see it in your face, you're excited. This is what you have been waiting to hear. This is why you first came to see me.

"All the voices of those who call writing a craft, who speak grammatically correct, who studied with this name or that one, well up in my head and tell me once again, each time I sit to do it, that I have no business doing what I'm doing. I don't have enough credits, awards, no Guggenheim, no South of France—New York poet in residence, nada, hombre. It's just me, desperately cutting an unknown path with a machete, trying not to remember, but writing it all down anyway.

"Too many have called me a tonta, una dummy, a brown spic india fea from the streets of a dirty city and left me there. Papi wanted five children from me, nothing else. 'Dummy,' he called me to my face one Christmas Eve when he had been drinking. I had just graduated from an Ivy League school.

"There are no laurels for the beauty or brilliance of a half-breed woman who doesn't play anybody's game. You can't buy it with charm as some might think; or solely be riding the wave of a trend that fortuitously defines who you are—as your embittered writing instructor has suggested of me—at least not for very long.

" 'What you need is a novio,' my widowed mother said to me on the phone the other day. She's afraid that my only having women friends, like my cousin Angie in Texas, means I've gone the other way. Who will be there to protect me—and my child, she worries. She has always worried that without a man I'll have no way to validate my existence. Any man will do. 'Get yourself a dishwasher,' she tells me. 'Don't aim so high!' "

You shake your head. And that little smile—that means what this time? You think I see you as the dishwasher? You already know too well the unshakable, ancient, double-standard expectations that Mexican mothers and fathers have of sons and daughters. Nothing I have said will help you write one word today or ever, give you the courage or confidence you need as a brown man and, in the end, it is the writing instructor with whom you feel the most empathy, whom you understand . . . Then you leave, closing the door quietly behind you.

I go to my desk.

◁ 17

"Tell me about a fantasy." We're in a dive in San Francisco. I am drinking margaritas out of a water glass. It is late afternoon and chilly. We will be leaving soon, and the rendezvous will be over.

"We'll have a church wedding, mariachis y todo."

"Will your family be there?"

"Of course!"

"And will your mother give the groom away to the bride?"

"Of course! And we'll even slaughter a pig!"

◁ 18

Once upon a long, long time ago, I was pregnant in Puerto Rico. I didn't know that I was pregnant. I only knew that every day that we were there—my mother and father, whole family—I was nauseous and I couldn't stay awake. I was sure I had come down with something—from all the community hours I'd put in all year, the little money I lived on, the poor diet I kept. My family went to Puerto Rico to attend a wedding and to visit relations, they made a rare invitation and I joined them.

One Saturday, the men brought a big, fat pig up to the house. Papi held it down while they slit its throat over a huge tub. On Sunday, we went to the country and had lechón. Well, at least the rest did. I slept through the picnic. I was pregnant and didn't know it yet. Months before, I had lost all pretenses to innocence. I didn't know then that perceiving me innocent was what the "father" had loved about me. Later, not because the innocence was gone or had ever been there, but simply when he realized I was not *innocent*, he began to be cruel to me—mocked me, belittled me at every turn, avoided me, took other women—despised me. I didn't know that my sin, my betrayal was that I had dared to love him in return.

◁ 19

Enough is enough.

"Tell me to stop loving you." It isn't fun anymore when the thought of coming apart from you will leave splinters in my side, my lips, nipples, soles of my feet. "Tell me, Apolinar, don't count on me." I put it another way still, "Tell me to blow you off."

"Why would I want to say a silly thing like that?" is all you ever answer when I tell you that.

◁ 20

Mami decided that the best thing was a divorce. Over fifteen years of his womanizing and her loneliness and working on the assembly line and the final straw was the day a new woman she was training at work told her that she knew Papi. She had worked with him at the plant where he was at that time. "No, it's impossible!" she told Mami. "Anastasio Espinoza can't be your husband!"

"But it's true!" Mami insisted—innocently. "Here is a picture of him. Here is a picture of our children . . . we've been married for sixteen years!"

"No—it's impossible!" The woman remained incredulous despite Mami's *proof.* "Anastasio—Nat Espinoza is not married. He lives with his mother. She's old and that's why no one can ever go to their house. But he is *living* with this Polish girl. They plan to get married. Moreover, there was this other woman, a Puerto Rican girl, at the plant. She even showed off the engagement ring he had given her! What a ruckus she raised at the factory the day she found out about the güera!"

◁ **21**

I've seen Mami drunk, smashed, completely loaded, twice in my life. The first time was at the end of that day. When I got home from work, she had a half-empty bottle of Cutty Sark in her hand. Papi's shirts were all laid out on the bed. When he got home, she was going to send him packing to the Polish girl.

The other time was the night before I left for Europe to do research on a book. I was going away for a month and I was leaving my fifteen-month-old infant in the care of his father, in her care, in the care of my whole family and a reliable babysitter—who was a friend and also cared. To her mind, I was abandoning my baby. Bad mother I was. Bad mother, bad wife. No-good woman.

That evening, over two decades ago, when Papi got home, he told Mami she was silly for listening to gossips. He put all his shirts back into the closet and sat down at the table for her to serve him his supper.

◁ **22**

Mami has given me a lot of bad advice. One example of inutile maternal guidance I've received is that no matter what was going on between my man and me, I should always have food prepared for him to eat whenever he got home. When I got wise that this was particularly bad advice, as innocent as it may appear, was a few years ago. I was waiting for my husband to come home. There was a young woman from out of town, a friend of friends of his. He was just being courteous, he said, picking her up at the airport, showing her around. I had baked a chicken for him, one of his favorite things. I have never liked to cook. The chicken was a desperate attempt to prevent a disaster already in progress. But they arrived together. I shouldn't have been surprised that he would invite her to our home. I wasn't surprised. What I felt instead was a tiny fire alarm going off inside. While I was getting the chicken out of the oven, he said to her, "Here, sit down. Have something to eat," pulling out a seat for her at the table, and she, waiting to be served, to be treated as a guest. The next evening he went out and didn't come home all night. The following morning, I too was gone.

◁ **23**

At this point, you are tempted, I'm sure, to take all this and neatly Freudian-analyze me to explain why after my marriage broke up I turned to women. Did you simply tolerate my feminist seminar to humor me, to find a way to be near me? Do you still think a woman's choice of a woman is in direct reaction to not being loved right by a man?

Not in the seminar and not when we have been alone have I ever felt at ease to discuss with you the intimacies between women. Women are no angels. Oh, we are no innocents. What we do when we are behind closed doors and the things we may say to one another and the horrendous violence that we can bring from the world to each other and make our own . . .

When I turn to women, when I have filled myself with Woman throughout my life—it is to remember that Eve was no betrayer. She was a sage holding on to humanity to save us all. But for the time being, she's been beaten.

▽ **24**

"I am so proud of you," Papi told me on his deathbed, holding my new book in his hand, impressed by its volume. Even writers are impressed with it unread, because of its size. "And I, of you," I said, holding the draft of a manuscript in my hand. He was dying and I was writing. Trying to figure it all out. The thing.

The guys who came to replace his oxygen supply were impressed with my new book, too. My mother showed them the others. "You wrote all those books?" they asked, smiling, kind of nervous and flustered in the presence of someone with so many words and the monkish discipline it must take to have put them all down. "Yeah," I heard one of them whisper to the other, "and so beautiful, too."

When they left, Papi's eyes were bright. "Did you see how impressed those guys were with your books?" I nodded. "I'm going to read this, as soon as I'm feeling a little better," he said. "Once I can get up and around again." Papi. He was going to read something I had written. Everybody was impressed. A big fat book with a glossy cover and my simple picture with the direct gaze on the back. Papi. Read what I wrote? Oh, my God. He, who had never given much consideration to the being who had sprung from the womb of a woman who had served him for forty years—and now, what would he think of the monster that I had become? And the thoughts that I have. The godless, female thoughts I have. And speak. And write. And what's more—people out there, important people, people in a position to publish are putting these thoughts out for the whole world to see.

◁ 25

"I hope I never get that disciplined about anything," you say. It is another breathless day in the tiny city by the azure sea, azure sky, azure melancholy welling up in our hearts after lunch—which today is the taquitos I fried up last night—reheated, with sour cream, and mango juice.

Go on, leave this place. I am leaving it soon, too. We have both paid our dues here, teacher and student. Take your thrift shop Remington to an island and type standing up as Hemingway did, or kneeling over the toilet in a cheap hotel, like Kerouac. You have your heroes ready-made.

"What will you think of me the next time you see me?" you asked me this morning when we teeter-tottered between forever-and-never-again-and-must-we-decide-now-this-moment-and-if-only-I-could-just-walk-away-how-much-easier-that-would-make-things-for-us-for-you-but-mostly-for-me.

"It all depends on what we say to each other when we part," I say, accepting that we are going to part, and more than this, not wanting to be with anyone who would want to part from me.

◁ 26

A few days after I left him, I got the call. Papi had called in a priest. I caught a plane within an hour and by that afternoon, I was with him at the hospital. "Don't let him see you cry," my sister told me just before I walked into his room. "Se nos va, hija," Mami, sitting by him, uttered, once I could let go of his hand, pull my lips away from his feverish brow. He is leaving us. "Papi, we have been so lucky knowing you," I whispered. I drove the rest of the family out; they were making too much noise, putting out too much weird energy, as they say in California. Many interminable hours passed. "What do you want, Papi?" I asked, close to his ear. His eyes were closed. We were alone. He was all mine. My charming, handsome, young father with the pianist's hands, too poor to learn to play the instrument of his choice, so when he did a short stint in a suitcase factory thirty years ago, he learned to sound out tones from the various cardboard suitcases, and he became a percussionist instead. I have his delicate thin-finger hands. I also did not get piano lessons. I would have preferred to do anything but this that I do which takes no more than a pencil and pad, and which is soundless and so without rhythm. "Do you want me to pray for you?" I asked, again in his ear. He shook his head, gasping heavily for his last breaths. "Get me . . . something . . . for the pain." I did. Papi died in his sleep.

◁ **27**

"I love, love to sleep with you," I have whispered to you some mornings when the sheets cling to us, and there's no point in getting up because all we can do is sleep, sleep together. "Why?" you ask me.

It feels like the first moments of birth, blindness, darkness, then departure from the moistness that is so safe and so infinitely, unquestionably protective. My twin embryo. Your body is like mine, angular. You snore a little. I get up a dozen times. I always come back to bed. Enclose you, thin but not brittle, limbs entwined like gnarled branches. I cannot explain anything about this between us, why you cried over me before knowing me, when I was still the writer to you, or why I invited you to my refuge when no one else was welcome, or why it feels like something has been fractured, an ankle bone, a wrist, when you go away for a couple of days, and why I always know you'll come back. I only know that sleeping eases the pain and then, the pain itself is not so horrible but becomes a crystal of translucent points through which I perceive all that exists and transcend my assembly-line life of words.

◁ **28**

"You have a daughter who has published a book and yet she got you working here," Papi told me a woman who also worked the graveyard shift at the factory once said to him, when he showed her my first collection of poems. Papi said he had only shrugged his shoulders. If I made money from my poems, he thought, it was my money, not his.

In the world of the factory, people equated books with money and money with freedom from the drill press, from losing fingers to brutal machinery, and from lazy foremen who tallied up your rates, threatened that without your quota tomorrow you would be bumped and out of a job by the end of the week altogether. Never mind that my book was of poems, a genre virtually considered worthless on the publishing market. It was a book and people who wrote books were important and important people had money.

Rare is the one who can love a poem for its own sake, show it off like a new hat, lick it clean like an ice-cream cone, who will cry over it like a son gone to war, talk with it, tell it all his secrets—share it with a friend. Rare—are you.

◁ **29**

"What will make you happy?" I asked that first weekend when you came unexpectedly and then did not leave.

"Truthfully? A poem."

I was so smitten with my new lover, who made me laugh, who had resurrected Nat as the restless young man who could not stop to think of a wife and children and baby daughter who had nothing to do with him except for having the same hands and since I had asked, I set upon the task of fulfilling that request. And once I gave you the poem, handwritten on a postcard of two lovers kissing, you showed it around. "Leave those women be!" your roommate ribbed you and you replied, not as long as you were serving as such inspiration.

"Here are two more," I said then. Poems on postcards: Tina Modotti's Mexican woman breastfeeding, another of a street photographer in Guatemala, a sign over his head that read, "Recuerdo." "And when you show these trophies off to your friend, tell him this," I said:

"If she were a seamstress, she would have stitched a shirt of pure silk, white as an angel's dream, with mother-of-pearl buttons, each eyelet hand-embroidered with silver thread— that I might parade around town, and the women think me handsome and the men think me rich.

"If she were a cobbler, she'd've fitted me for boots, up to the knee, patent leather and color of burgundy. Like a gaucho of Patagonia I'd primp and stride about. And no one would ever notice I don't own so much as a horse!

"If she were a cook (and of course, this is not so far-reaching but no, she doesn't even like to cook), she would have prepared a feast like those served the emperor before the fall of Tenochtitlán—a feast of turkey and chiles, roasted esquintle and chocolate, enough to feed all the palace but forbidding anyone to touch a morsel before I was done, washed, and taking my siesta.

"But no, this one only writes verses. They are useless. They can't shelter you against the wind, satisfy your stomach's yearning. You cannot gamble with them when you've lost your money, your coat, or your shoes. Who would give a dime for a poem? No, she is only a poet of sorts. Moreover, verses come easy to her. She is a woman, after all."

◁ 30

Your mother was locked up in her room on her wedding night by her husband while he went out carousing, you said, and began to weep. Imagine that life! you cried. A good Mexican son crying over his sacred, suffering mother's life, bearing too many children, enduring a fallen womb, cancer of the uterus from birth control, and the husband who never thought her good enough for him.

My sister was beaten on the street on her wedding night by her groom, the man to whom she has been married now for twenty-five years. His whole family looked on. I alone jumped on him to try to make him stop.

My cousin has had seven children. She is not allowed to have visitors. She does not have a telephone. Her husband has kept her hidden for nearly twenty years.

I could have told you these stories, but you did not want to hear about other women. Your mother is the only woman that matters. The things I will never talk about or write, I sum up and say, "I once led the life of a dog." You say nothing.

◁ 31

You, at twenty-three, loverboy, have never been left, you say. Your family members, mother, father, each one intact. Except through death, I too have not been left before. We announce this to each other, like two opponents in the ring, as if to leave were a victory of some sort, even through death. Would it not be more triumphant to say, I stayed? I simply loved and did not want to leave. Leaving is for the defeatist, the egotist, the one who is not worthy of the love he or she rejected.

Perhaps not.

Like you, I adored my life, lavished myself with its sweet aroma, shamelessly derived pleasure from sheer existence. Therefore, also like you, I thought I would be punished by our jealous Mexican Catholic God and die young. I dreamt of it frequently as an adolescent. My father had also been so much this way, and though he did not die young, he did not die old. Once, when he was the age I am now, after an evening of beers, slumped in a chair, he began to sob arrantly, "I don't want to die. I am afraid of dying." He went on like that before passing out.

He died unresigned to death. he had loved his life so, just breathing, long after the adventures, lovers, and highs were behind him. Without a job, or great comforts, he attached himself to the petty things of his surroundings, the novelty of the VCR, new CD player, neighbors he got on with and even those with whom he didn't and those surviving lifelong friends. His desire to stay had nothing to do with any inability to leave anyone. Although I had been with him, holding his hand, wiping his brow, keeping the oxygen mask in place, ceaselessly for six hours, he did not say goodbye, so much as raise his hand in a father's blessing. Instead, he asked me to open the hermetically sealed hospital windows, to open the door wider. Air. All that he wanted and needed on that winter night before dying was air.

◁ **32**

"You are earth and air and sky to me," I wrote in my first verse to you. And I, in turn, have become what? Rock and stone, sediment and ash. The poet who was never a poet but a sharpshooting female who blew men off like cans off a tree stump came home to bury her father. She took the money she had earned from the poems that had been written for him and bought his coffin.

She went with her mother and sister to pick out two plots, one for the mother, next to the father's, located next to a large statue of St. Peter. "When I die, Silvia," she asked her sister, suddenly all too aware that no matter how far she traveled away from these people she was bound to by blood, they would own her, "just cremate me, okay? Don't fuss over me. Don't go to any expense. It's not worth it."

Her elder sister, the good Catholic, stared, horrified at the extent of her sister's sacrilege. "Get away from me," she responded. "You're going to burn in hell and take me with you."

"No, Silvia," the poet protested (as poets are wont to do whenever on the subject of death), "you don't understand. You will only go to hell, if you believe in hell."

"Well, I do."

"Well, then, *you're* in big trouble."

◁ **33**

The sun has begun to set. I cannot see them from here, from these dark rooms that I have inhabited for the past ten months, more transient I've become than traveler, but I know the voluminous clouds are hovering over the mountain peaks. There will be no fog tonight.

I have opened up the wine. I've gone back to smoking cigarettes. I think that sometime tonight you'll come back, not because you want to, would not prefer the company of your friends, former classmates, all of you preparing to set off on your lives, when everything is left to that wide expanse of the future. We believe we are moving in a straight line when in fact we travel in spirals all our lives—so wide, at first, that for a long time we've thought we were heading forward. But after years, decades perhaps, the spirals have begun to narrow, finally, become ringlets of echo and memory.

That is when you will come back—a man in a ringlet of fire.

◁ 34

Every night without fail, after his death I dreamt of him as an aberration. I knew he was dead but I would have him back any way I could. Sometimes I dreamed I was without feet, learning to walk on crutches, to adapt myself to this condition without him. One night or morning the dreams stopped. Then one night, not long after, you came by. You looked around. Out of vanity or desire or simply needing a place to crash, you announced, "This feels like home. You should let me come live with you."

◁ 35

It was a long time since I talked to a man, in the twilight, in shadows, kissed his hands, heard his secrets, told him my own. Don't turn on the light, you warn me when you cry. Otherwise, you become bullyish, resentful of me if I catch a glimpse of your tears.

The night of his thirty-fifth birthday so many years ago, after he left Annette's apartment on his own (after we'd gone), he met us at his brother's house, where a birthday party in his honor had been planned and we were waiting. Shortly after he arrived, to funereal silence, he began to cry. "Comfort your father," my mother, who did not move from her spot, ordered me. "You are so cold. She has always been so cold," she told my uncle and the other guests as if I weren't there. "Put your arms around him." She insisted, "Tell him to come home . . ."

◁ **36**

Sometimes, I forget and think he is still making plans to visit this summer. I long for his voice on the telephone, that easy manner of his, the vacant, repeated promise of "If there's anything you need, I'm here." I asked you this morning, "And when I go through the tunnel, this thing so popularly known these days as the process, when I write what I must write, not what I want to or how I wish I could write, not what anyone will necessarily want to read for any reason, just what I've needed to write—tell me you'll be on the other end. Tell me you'll say something simple like, 'Apolinar, let's go for a walk on the beach,' or 'Time to eat, let's go get a taco.' Remind me that I am still part of this world." *If there's anything you need, I'm here.*

Instead you kissed me, just as you always do before leaving. I tasted on your lips, your tongue, the acrid isolation of each man and woman and knew then that you would not come back, no matter what.

◁ Foreign Market

At the market he calls out something—especially directed at her, she senses. But she does not understand what he has said. She turns around. He smiles. His eyes are succulent as oranges and very black and his smile has made her forget about the cold. He says something again, to her, momentarily he has thought that they are compatriots, from their dark skin despite mid-winter and black hair, but when she does not reply again, he realizes his mistake. He's not embarrassed; still, they are both foreigners, outsiders. She is not interested in apples or potatoes which he points to, coyly directing his succulent eyes to the weight hanging overhead. She begins to go on her way. But he calls to her again. He puts out a hand, wait, hold on, a universal signal facile to understand and she does.

Later they are warming up with a café crème in a café down the boulevard. They get acquainted by writing to each other on a napkin, a pictograph-numerology revelation of vital statistics. She is thirty. She is very old, she thinks, but only writes "30." He smiles and writes "22." Now she is certain that she is old. But he puts a chafed hand, that has been out at the market since before dawn, carrying bushels and crates, spraying the sidewalk in the cold, behind her neck and draws her head to him for an abrupt kiss. He looks around and points at the cinema down the street. He turns to her questioningly and she nods. Yes, they can go to the movies. Why not?

It is four in the afternoon.

In the dark theater they act like teenagers and never watch the movie. He puts her hand on him.

She is thinking, she is thirty and left her husband and child three weeks ago. She has come to this city, this famous city, scandalously famous, because a good friend lives here now, and because it is so far away from her life that she thought she could think things through.

He walks her back to the apartment. In the entranceway, they kiss like parting lovers. He fondles her. The concierge's door is slightly ajar, then slams shut. The pretend lovers say goodbye and promise to meet at the market at two in the afternoon on Saturday. Yes, they can figure that much out using the national lingua, two on Saturday.

That evening her friend says (she is surprised at her friend's response), "Are you serious? You can't be serious! You met him at the market! I could see an Arab you met at the embassy but this one works as a vendor . . . ! He has no money to speak of . . . You really can't be serious!"

On Saturday, punctually, she arrives at his stall. At first he appears too busy to stop. He weighs onions and mushrooms by the kilo and has hardly acknowledged her, although he has seen her. She takes a seat on a crate nearby. After a quarter of an hour and he has made no attempt to communicate, no hand gesture at all, avoids eye contact, turns to his comperes and speaks in his language, says something she does not understand but is embarrassed by anyway, she gets up to leave.

The boulevard is very wide and very long and it seems it is taking her an eternity to walk away. Then someone calls her. He is calling her by name. She does not recognize the voice but she still hopes it is him, and she turns around. It is one of the comperes. He is older. His wavy, blondish-red hair is mostly covered with a wool cap. Wait! he signals and she does. It is even colder than it was the other day. Perhaps he is bringing a message. She huddles and watches her breath stream out of her nose. When they are face to face, he says, almost supplicating, that *he* can go with her. Catching on, she shakes her head firmly and turns off. He calls her again— wait, please! She picks up her pace, the click-click of her boots sharp and fast on the asphalt, faster, faster.

◁ SUBTITLES

i have lived my life in a foreign film. Black and white mostly. Fassbinderish, i think. Having spoken one language in the five-room-flat secluded world of my grandmother until the age of six when i was sent to foreign film school—

Hushhhh. i whispered the new language in fragmented sentences that jutted out of my mouth like broken glass caught in my throat. The first day when my older sister left me there, startled by the sudden appearance of subtitles at my feet, i ran out of the classroom.

i did enormously better than others back then, however, i have come to realize, while exchanging these early foreign film stories. Better than my old friend, Juana, who was sent to the class for the hearing impaired for being unable to handle the subtitles. She did not learn the new language, she tells me. But she did become quite adept at signing.

In my school, however, there would have been no such luck. There was one alternative class alone, where all children who challenged their teachers for reasons not restricted to language difficulties were banished to until they were old enough to drop out of school, six-year-olds with sixteen-year-olds: The Dumb Bell Room.

i, on the other hand, was not a foreigner—i was living in a foreign film. Typecast at times, especially during those formative years in the vast expanse of the inner city—caught between African-American children with Mississippi accents and gypsy adult-like children who simply had no use for school at all after the second grade.

Miscast during what may have been the bloom of my womanhood except for the fact that a renegade does not bloom so much as explode.

But later, oh finally, much later, i ascended with tenacity and confidence to the illustrious heights of stardom. And a star can be anything she wants.

So here i am. New casting. This is not a set. We are filming this scene on location. Spare no expense. And who would have ever thought . . . ?

Passing through the music department. i am not six in this scene but thirty-eight now. The students, the professors are all foreign, of course. Yet, what is beautiful about all this, what was once so tormenting and now is the very source for my celebrity EVERYWHERE i go is that *i* am the one who is cast forever foreign. There is Mozart playing in the halls and the women are natural blonds. They appraise my Chichicastenango huipil. i smile at their naked stares. My dark fingers, rimmed with gold, reach up to my collarbone to rub the Virgen de Guadalupe/Tonantzin talisman medal that hangs from a thin gold chain.

i live, you understand, in a foreign film.

i have cultivated a disturbing but sensuous foreign accent like Ingrid Bergman's.

i don't always wear huipiles from Chichicastenango, Xela, or Mitla. i usually show off spandex pants embroidered with silver roses, or a silk raincoat or Djuna Barnes red lipstick and wide-brimmed hat or Marlene Dietrich waves or Katherine Hepburn shoulders or a Greta Garbo cleft and i don't mean on the chin.

It is so hard to be original.

María Sabina, Oaxacan shamaness peyote spell caster, suits my "type" best. If you can't be original, at least you can be complex.

i never disappoint my devoted public.

Traveling, not with bruja wings but on trains and jets to places María Sabina would not go, i find myself led to a place of foreignness of greater proportions than those created by the original script.

Behind a closed door at the end of the hall i recognize *Don Giovanni* on the piano. It is the only opera i have ever attended. A fortuitous coincidence for me who can now turn casually to my host and smile: "Ah, *Don Giovanni!*" And he smiles back because the bridge i made by composition recognition makes him less uneasy with this unsolicited confrontation with otherness.

We reach the reception salon.

A dried flower arrangement at the center of the table. Domestic champagne. Platters of fruit and cheese. The usual.

Someone introduces herself and whispers in my ear. i throw my head back, laughing, a thousand rays of light radiate from the center of my being à la María Sabina.

The cinematographer moves in for a close-up.

i have no lover. Neither on location nor back at the studios where my life is usually filmed. Another detail to note. It is certain to be relevant to the development of the plot.

Someone says in that pseudo-confident tone that ambitious people from general casting use in such scenes (nothing short of bad acting if you ask me), *"She's a lesbian, you know."*

The other extra, the one who has become involuntarily privy to this new information, strains her neck a bit, scrutinizes the star to see if she can determine this for herself:

Beneath the huipil, sheer black stockings with seams.

Red manicured fingernails.

Have we entered Monika Treut territory?

The protagonist is still laughing. Definitely not "Seduction: The Cruel Woman" material, the observer concludes of the star who is still doing María Sabina with a little bit of Nastassja Kinski.

We are into something only marginally Hollywood here. More along the lines of the Canadian metis-feminist genre, if there is one. A cross between *Loyalties* and *Getting a Winter Tan*, maybe.

Another nobody-extra offers: "Actually, if she takes off that costume, she has breasts."

Big breasts?

It is all a matter of perspective. The cinematographer's.

I like her earrings. Detail is the director's forte. They are gold, of course, tiny Mayan masks.

Clues to her origin? Or just more visual effect to dazzle the viewer, like the little espresso coffeepot earrings on that weirdly beautiful actress in Almodovar's *fabulously* successful *Woman on the Verge* . . . ?

Espresso is very European. Indian mask gold earrings are very American . . .

Indian from America. Where Columbus arrived, not where he was headed, but insisted that the inhabitants were Indian anyway.

Indigenous mask earrings cast from an original Mayan mold. You can count on that. Except that the originals were ear-plugs, going through the lobe in a much larger hole than the needle-thin one fashionable today. Holes were drilled into the teeth then as well, for adorning purposes. Embedded with precious gems. Trendsetters those people were.

She is smiling gold and turquoise.

And starts to laugh again.

It is the domestic champagne. And the accent is getting thicker. Before you know it, she'll be speaking Mixtec.

She is not an actor.

She is not in costume.

She was born inside this film.

Her mother, who had birthed all her other children at home, was forced to a hospital with this last one. She gave her new-born daughter's name to the nun-nurse who immediately translated it. And thus, her career began.

Sometimes she cooks things, our star, but from no particular native cuisine. Yes, yes, she does mother-learned and grand-mother-cherished recipes very well. She also does pesto and quiche with molcajete and metate. *Very* American, you know.

What isn't American these days with Gary Snyder declaring himself among the "New Indians of America"?

From across the room you can see that strange light emitting from her belly button.

What if she were Chinese? But of course not, too tall.

Not too tall. What is it then?

She just isn't. Anyone can tell that. And you can't Anthony Quinn her into it, either.

She stops laughing, now sizing up the man with the full head of white hair and neatly trimmed beard and assessing a potential development of the plot here. He could bring her gifts like St. Nick. Not just at Christmas.

Sometimes it's so hard to take her seriously.

She begins to fuss with her little Guatemalan change purse, the kind that is popular with Californian students these days, and pulls out two little photographs, passes them around.

Everyone who examines them smiles politely, hands them to someone else. They are of a child who is a very small version of herself.

The child is away at school, she says.

Ah, of course.

Very bright, she says. Gets only the highest marks. Very sociable, too. Makes friends with everyone.

Of course.

He is going to be an artist when he grows up.

Oh? (Polite laughter here from those around her.)

Like his mother, she adds. And laughs again, putting the little photos that have been passed between index finger and thumb all around back into the little bag.

She has very thick, very black hair. It is natural.

Each time she laughs, either because of the champagne or because this is the only direction she has received so far in this scene, she runs her thin gold-rimmed fingers through the front of her hair. Gold with a pearl. Gold with black onyx. Gold and a diamond.

"You must catch the 19:04," someone alerts her. "The trains here are usually punctual."

"Yes, yes, don't worry!" she responds, almost flirtatiously although she didn't notice who in the crowd has spoken to her. It's certainly the champagne causing this sudden transformation of character. It doesn't make her giddy, but she would never smile provocatively without the champagne, which is not a prop, but real.

The gathering is in her honor.

She is come to avenge the Conquest.

Don't make cheap-shot Aztec jokes like: Will she cut any hearts out for an encore?

Of course, she will cut hearts out.

Just don't say it.

Don't ask if she will make it rain, either.

Maybe she will just do something mundane, like stare a bull down, later, in the scenes where she is resting in the countryside.

She reaches over to the table and with a silver pick helps herself to a piece of sheep cheese.

Cheap cheese?

She repeats with her accent which is like the cheese the locals have cultivated a certain taste for. The cheese is transported from Yugoslavia, unlike sheep milk, which obviously sheep produce, to suckle baby sheep of course, and for Yugoslavs to produce cheese cheaply for export.

Enough of the cheese, and the strawberries too, cut into precise quarters to skirt the crystal platters.

Who will she sacrifice first?

The cast, for the most part, except for those cynics who would have guessed it, is unaware of her plan. Everyone is directed to move about the room, mingle cocktail-party style, and assume that they have it all under control.

She is laughing a little again and you can see the ray of light from her center but cannot hear any sounds from her mouth. Kind of early Buñuel. Everyone appears oblivious and content.

Now, if she did have a lover, would it be a man lover?

The receptionists hold out their long-stemmed glasses to the new bottle of champagne (no, you cannot say "receptionists" for those attending a reception—they are guests, simply guests) and toast to the Receiver. (And she is not a "Receiver," but the guest of honor.)

Translation is a vastly unappreciated art form.

If she does get a man lover on location or in this film at all, she wants him to have one of these strange names the people have here. They are ugly-sounding, actually, as if describing an organ transplant or a root canal operation, or a food one wouldn't necessarily like to eat but surprisingly finds delicious, like cow brains or tongue.

But the men, apart from their names, are not necessarily ugly or morbid in any apparent way, despite their Transylvanian accents, and she feels very certain that she could acquire a taste for one of them.

The women are much too tall for her liking, so they have all been dismissed. She doesn't see herself wearing Humphrey Bogart elevated shoes for the kissing scenes.

Engaging suddenly in an anarchy of mini-melodramas, the supporting cast has begun to drift off. "Try to remember why we are all here, people!" the director shouts through the megaphone. "At least *act* like you're interested!"

She is looking a little tired suddenly. Makeup! Makeup! Where the hell is that makeup person?

Full shot as she abruptly exits and hurries down the hall toward the lift.

Somebody stop her!

"i want to be alone," i say in a low tone.

"What?" "What did she say?" "What is it?"

"I'M GETTING MY PERIOD!" i shout. No one has directed me to say this, but i occasionally indulge my diva tendencies. Although with no-talent culture appropriators like Madonna and Cher out there, what can you really do for shock effect these days, anyway? This, however, does freeze the cast, and the cinematographer and director, for the moment, let me go.

If you want to be alone, try living in an adobe in the desert. No one, with the exception of an occasionally unwelcome rattlesnake or coyote, comes to visit, not even my child. My only human contact being when i go to the plaza to work out three times a week for two hours. Unlike celebrity sellouts, i cannot afford a private trainer and have to join the locals at the jazzercise class at the YMCA. It's hard to have a great body, Raquel Welch said recently, and she ought to know. While Rita Moreno, who made a big-time debut voluptuously dancing around to "I Want to Be in America," now advertises her excerise video looking like a bulimic, along with the *Klute* radical, who seems to have started this all, forgoing international politics for staying in shape and making movies about foreigners. Victoria Principal, who looks foreign but is not, scammed a $300,000 advance for her exercise book and i suppose you could own your own trainer with that kind of money. But then, in a way not greatly advertised but brought out in a Barbara Walters interview for sure, she built a whole career based on scamming.

i do my own wax jobs, too.

Although there was a time when i definitely went au naturel. No, not in the sixties. Contrary to popular belief, i was not a flower child radical. In 1968 i was thirteen years old and playing an African American with a huge reddish-brown Afro wig, because the last thing i wanted to play then was hippie and white.

And Martin Luther King was an American Gandhi at my school.

But being neither black nor white invalidated my existence.

And even without the wig, back in the Godfather Lounge on the South Side of Chicago, where i used to sneak in with false IDs, people saw the long, straight hair and would ask incidentally of my Black and Proud look, "Do you have a little Indian blood?"

A little?

East Indian, maybe? Barbados?

i am Coatlicue.

But no, not then, not yet. Then i was only a neophyte stone fertility filth-eating goddess. Not when i left the long black hair on my legs and underarms either, although yes, there i was, being something hard to pinpoint again, Muslim-looking perhaps, with the nosepin and the occasional sari.

No one knew how to cast me then. i may have been up for a dozen Oscars but for the fact that exotic types were rarely appreciated for their acting. It was just assumed that i was doing what came naturally to being Other, and obedient to rote training—like Bonzo or Lassie. And to my knowledge neither of them was ever nominated either, despite the fact that one co-starred with a minor actor who became president of the country.

And how grateful i should have been for the pats on the head, but no, surely my unrefined breeding had something to do with my Marlon Brando temperament, insufferable and sulking, a complete anti-social, not to mention fatality incarnated to anyone who attempted intimacy—back then.

i could not stand the very idea of anyone who belonged in the movie stealing the scene, feeling too comfortable with her or his part, assuming i would eventually be moved off the set, dismissed. And more than a few did more than assume. "Get rid of her!" they demanded of the director. "She's got no training! Doesn't know a damn thing about Shakespeare!"

But who was doing Shakespeare? Surely none of them. Cecil B. DeMille convinced no one that Charleton Heston could really part the Red Sea nor did Otto Preminger's fresh discovery Jean Seberg make much of a Joan of Arc—although ironically, she was burned at the stake in the movie of her life for being prophetic and unable to save her country, or rather, forbidden to do so, as happened to Joan.

In the desert i do not worry about honing my accent, nor about my image. There isn't even a vague attempt at personal style. No makeup. Hair pulled back. In the plaza i look like any of the unemployed or underemployed women who stock their family pantries with 89-cent 32-ounce colas, dried chili powder, and blue-corn atole in a box, who drive a 4 x 4, and who marginally maintain a fifteen-year marriage to a man who wears a baseball cap to cover a receding hairline and has a name like Santiago.

i look like any of them, but i am not any of them.

i drive a red sports car with a license plate that reads: TOL-TECA. i wear a gold-plated Gucci watch—sent to me by a secret admirer, of course—nouveau-richely to the supermarket where i buy my cola and atole. i drink brandy with supper and listen to Astor Piazolla on my tape player as i cruise up I-40.

It comes with the territory of being a self-made star.

i have earned an unflattering local reputation for snubbing would-be suitors of either gender and being very particular about friendships in general. Stars are tolerated around here but not the self-assurance that often comes with their renown. But snubbing is not exactly based on snobbery. i would snub even if i were not famous. i tolerate very few people, which is why i moved alone to the desert, but cannot have enough of the world—whether it is the opera or this desert, with its dust and tumbleweeds. The constant drone of the cicadas. The sweat cupped beneath my breasts when i sit perfectly still in the shade. The sound of the hard rain at night.

In a foreign film everything, inanimate and otherwise, is an object, a prop. But in the desert, especially at night with the rain, no one directs me to throw back my head and laugh. No one is intimidated by the light that radiates from my center. No one knows what i dream when i lie in the middle of an empty room on a futon and close my eyes to the spider-webs that connect between vigas on the ceiling. The dreams are yet another film, less foreign than the one i live in out there, that you, dear public, need only spend an hour or so viewing, while i must continue inventing and reinventing my roles until death, for the sake of your entertainment.

◁ LA MISS ROSE

Wh=hen she first saw Miss Rose she was startled.
The bad eye, which Miss Rose made no attempt to cover with
a patch or dark glasses, kept staring at her and Carmen didn't
know which way to turn. "Stormy suggested that you might
be able to help me," Carmen told her, looking away and trying
not to stare back at the eye.

People around town thought that Miss Rose was very exotic,
being from a place called the "West Indies" and wearing a
purple scarf around her head. She had her nose pierced. How
she ended up at the edge of the desert was anybody's guess.

Stormy, who was on personal terms with la Miss Rose, said
Miss Rose was from Arkansas.

"Miss Rose can help anybody, darling, come in. Sit down
and tell me how Miss Rose can help you today," Miss Rose
told Carmen.

She had led Carmen to a room that was like those she had
seen belonging to fortune tellers on TV, a round table covered
with a printed fringed scarf. There was a crystal ball in the
center, wrapped in purple silk. Also on the table was what

Carmen presumed to be a deck of tarot cards. Miss Rose sat on a high-backed old cushioned chair and Carmen took the other, which was a kitchen chair and not very comfortable.

"Oh." Carmen started to feel a little shy for some reason. "It's about love . . . I'm sure everyone wants to know about love."

"Lots of people do, baby. But lots of people want to know about other things too, like how to make a lot of money. I have helped many people become very successful in their business by just following my advice. Now who is she?"

Carmen stared at Miss Rose for a moment, trying to concentrate on the good eye. "Actually, it's a he," she said.

"Hmm," Miss Rose said, not really embarrassed by her presumption because she was going to stand by what she *saw*. "I had this feeling about you that you liked women."

"I do like women . . . very much," she said, but she wanted to get to the point. She did not know if the meter on the hour she paid for a consultation with Miss Rose was already running but she wanted to make the most of it.

"Yeah, I thought so!" Miss Rose said and suddenly she was laughing. "Yeah, I thought so!" she said again and shook a finger at Carmen as if Carmen had been trying to pull her leg.

"I used to be married to a Spanish girl, you know," Miss Rose said. "She ran away with someone else . . ."

Carmen knew what Miss Rose meant by "Spanish." She spoke Spanish but she was not Spanish, which of course might mean a person from Spain but she had always thought that the word for that person was a Spaniard. Still, she knew what la Miss Rose meant. And still, she wanted to get to the point.

Miss Rose was looking at Carmen. "Does *he* know about your *true* connection with women?"

Carmen shrugged her shoulders. She wondered why Miss Rose didn't know the answer herself. She looked down at the crystal ball. She looked up at Miss Rose. "I don't know," she said. She was beginning to get impatient.

"There's a place just outside of town, has hot tubs, nice rooms with sundecks, just for women. Do you know about it?" Miss Rose asked. Carmen shook her head. "If you'd like, we could go there sometime . . . you, me, invite Stormy, too."

Carmen liked women. She did not like Miss Rose, however. She did not particularly like her gynecologist, nor the dental hygienist she went to either, who were also women. To her mind, they were just people she went to to perform a service for her for which she paid, like this Miss Rose. "Miss Rose, I would like to know what you 'see' with regards to my friend. We are not speaking to each other right now and I would really like to know what I should do about it."

Miss Rose looked a little disappointed and reluctantly motioned for Carmen to put her hands out. Miss Rose began to study Carmen's palms. "Hmm," she said, "hmm." Miss Rose looked up. With a slight push of Carmen's hands, as if dismissing them, Miss Rose leaned back.

"I see three Spanish men coming into your life very soon," Miss Rose declared.

Carmen turned away. Her eyes wandered outside the window next to her and landed on the people across the street standing outside the barbershop. She counted. One, two, three "Spanish men," all talking, or men who were not "Spanish" but who were perhaps talking in Spanish. "Hmm," she said. Then she turned back to la Miss Rose. "Don't you see my friend at all?"

"What do you mean?"

"My friend, the one I was seeing?"

"Isn't he Spanish?"

Carmen sighed. She was really going to have to talk with Stormy about this Miss Rose. "No," she said.

"No," Miss Rose replied. "But Miss Rose can fix something up for you. I have all kinds of powders. I mix them up myself. You want one special, I can fix it up for you today."

"I've tried powders," Carmen told Miss Rose. Actually, she had not been the one to try powders but remembered her friend, Pancha, who had committed a faux pas spell. She accidentally spilled a little pink love attraction powder on an envelope of a letter she was sending to a married man who would not leave her alone. In the letter she told him (for the third time since he had started to pursue her) to leave her alone or she would tell his wife. But the pink powder made things worse. After that, he would not leave her alone at all and Pancha ended up having to tell the man's wife about him. It was not a happy ending.

Carmen did not want to fool with powders.

"Anything else?" she asked Miss Rose, although she did not expect anything at all by then.

Miss Rose looked rather uninterested in Carmen's inquiry. Actually, she seemed annoyed by it. "You know, Miss Rose is really very tired today, darling, but if you would like, I could give you some powders," Miss Rose said again.

"No, I don't want powders," Carmen said again, too, and wondered why she was starting to sound apologetic. "I just wondered if you could tell me something about my friend."

"Does he love you?" Miss Rose asked.

Carmen stared expressionlessly at Miss Rose.

"Because if he doesn't love you, honey, you don't need him. You know that's the mistake that a lot of people make. They give their love to the wrong people. Like that Spanish girl I married. I gave her everything, but she just wasn't ready to settle down. She didn't appreciate a good thing. You know what I mean?"

"Well . . . ," Carmen said, "maybe, she'll come back when she does."

"No, no! I don't want her back, now! After all I did for her? I bought her beautiful clothes, beautiful furniture for our apartment, everything new. I treated her with a lot of class. A fifty-dollar blouse once. You know what I mean, don't you? And she took everything . . . *everything*, I tell you. I came home one day and the whole place was empty. Empty. She met this other woman and they both took off together . . . with everything!"

"Did you call the police?"

"No, no!" Miss Rose said, shaking her head and straightening her scarf. "I didn't want to bring no trouble to the girl. You understand. I still loved her and all. She was just too young."

"How old was she?"

"She was just too young for that kind of commitment and to appreciate what I was offering her," Miss Rose said. She took out a pouch and began to roll a joint.

Carmen slipped on her jacket and got up to leave. Miss Rose offered Carmen a toke on the joint and Carmen shook her head. "Look, baby," la Miss Rose said, with the smoke still somewhere in her throat, "forget that man. If he's giving you a hard time, you don't need him."

"I know that," Carmen said, "I just thought you might see something . . . "

Miss Rose shook her head. "It's a bad day for Miss Rose," she said. "Sometimes Miss Rose needs a little time . . . to get to know a person, to see their aura and to be able to feel things. You know what I mean?"

Carmen nodded. She sat back down. "He wasn't treating me bad," she felt inclined to defend herself, to separate herself from Miss Rose as a scorned woman.

"Nobody should treat anybody bad," Miss Rose said. Carmen nodded and stood up again to leave.

"Wait, let me give you something." Miss Rose got up and went to her altar which was filled with *a lot* of *stuff*. She put something in Carmen's hand. It was a small medal of Santa Barbara made out of something dull like tin. "I don't like to see my clients go away without anything to remember Miss Rose by!" She looked a little disappointed when Carmen showed no appreciation of the gesture and simply slipped the medal into her jacket pocket without a word.

"Don't forget, sugar! I can help you with making money, if you want. Miss Rose has helped more than one businessman make a fortune. People come back to me all the time. They say, 'Miss Rose, thank you so much! You saved our business!' They send me expensive presents and they are just so grateful for Miss Rose. I can mix up powders for you, baby, and oils for a bath, too, if you like. You just tell Miss Rose what you need, you'll see. Miss Rose can change your life. Next time you come back to see Miss Rose . . ."

◁ An Abrupt Encounter with La Miss Rose

Well, how are *you* this morning! Here! Look what I have, a present for you, *baby*!" La Miss Rose handed a small fancy department store bag to Carmen. Bright pink tissue stuck out. It looked like an Easter basket.

It was quite sunny out but la Miss Rose wasn't wearing sunglasses. She was squinting with her good eye. "I'm on my way to have my hair done," she said, running the index finger of each hand around the rim of her turban. "I think I'll have a perm done," she added. No one had ever seen la Miss Rose's hair.

"And what about me, Miss Rose? Don't I get a good morning today?" Stormy asked.

"Oh, of course Miss Rose wishes you a good morning, too, baby! Look, I have a present for you, too! Erzulie La Belle Vénus wants us all to smell as lovely as we are!" Miss Rose leaned over and gave Stormy a quick hug and then handed her the other little bag she was carrying which looked just like the one she gave Carmen.

Carmen and Stormy were seated at a white wrought-iron table at an outdoor café, the only café in town. They were both holding their presents up. They smiled at la Miss Rose and then at each other.

"Come over and let Miss Rose read your cards sometime!" Miss Rose said to Stormy.

"Yes. I've been meaning to do that, Miss Rose," Stormy said. Around Miss Rose, Stormy, the former stripper, for some reason acted like a schoolgirl.

"Well, ladies, I'm off to get my hair done," Miss Rose said and left. Stormy and Carmen watched Miss Rose walk down the hot street.

"Well, what do you think it is . . . they are?" Carmen asked Stormy.

"I don't know. Let's look," Stormy said. She licked a bit of strawberry jam from her fingertips and then plunged her hand into the bag. She pushed the tissue around and pulled out a square gift-wrapped box. Like the tissue paper, it was covered with the product's designer's initials. Carmen watched Stormy open the box.

"It's a soap," Stormy said. Stormy had not gotten a gift in a long time.

Carmen reached in less enthusiastically than Stormy and seeing that it was identical in shape and size as Stormy's box concluded it was also soap. Stormy took out her soap and sniffed it through the plastic seal. "Umm," she said, "smells good, like vanilla!"

"Are you going to use it?" Carmen asked, looking at her box which lay unopened on the corner of the table. Carmen took a sip of her coffee as if she were being watched by her box.

"Hell yeah!" Stormy said. "This stuff is expensive! It smells pretty good, too!"

"Who is Erzulie?" Carmen wondered aloud. Stormy shrugged her shoulders and avoided eye contact. If she knew, for some reason she wasn't telling.

"Is Erzulie some kind of goddess?" Carmen insisted. "Why does she want us to smell good?"

Stormy shrugged her shoulders again and began to look restless. Overall, Stormy was a restless woman. The surprise soap and Miss Rose's abrupt appearance had already lost their glow.

"What do you think of Miss Rose's card readings?" Carmen tried again. Carmen, on the other hand, lived alone, talked rarely, and dwelled and dwelled for long spells of time in her head.

"I think her powders are better," Stormy said, putting down her soap and picking up her buttered scone. "But then again, now that I think about it, maybe I shouldn't say that."

"Hmm," Carmen said. She lifted up her sunglasses and squinted. Way down the street was a little Miss Rose, still walking.

"Where do you think she's headed?" Carmen asked.

"To get her hair done is what she said," Stormy answered. She took her soap and put it carefully back into the Easter basket bag.

"I heard her," Carmen said. "But look at her way down

there." Wherever it was that la Miss Rose was headed, there wasn't a shop for miles.

Stormy turned for a second, for Carmen's benefit. She couldn't have spotted Miss Rose just like that but still she said, "Yeah, I know. La Miss Rose doesn't drive."

◁ MAYBE MÉNAGE, MAYBE JUST LUNCH

The sky was covered with a magenta sash. Behind it Erzulie the Virgin, Grande St. Anne, and their daughter Xochiquetzal were having a wienie roast. The coals tipped over and set the sky on fire. Great elephant clouds stampeded toward Santa Fe. The sky was always busy.

Both Stormy and Miss Rose accepted Carmen's invitation to visit her in her little adobe with the cactus sprawling yard that her anal hedge-lawn neighbors hated. Every week the city received an anonymous complaint from a community resident about Carmen's yard.

Although it was rare, every now and then Carmen acknowledged that human company was good. But it had taken weeks before she called either woman. In truth, there was a lot Carmen wanted to know about la Miss Rose and a lot she wished she didn't know about Stormy.

Carmen served her guests tea, not Earl Grey or Star of Anis, but Cota. She had picked it herself while hiking that morning in the nearby Manzano Mountains. Stormy, who claimed she had quit drinking, pulled out a half pint of Seagram's from her gym bag. She could not stomach tea by itself, she told Carmen, and spiked her cup of tea, good Cota or not.

"What else do you carry in that gym bag?" Carmen asked.

"A lot of things, honey. Everything a cab driver needs to get through the night." Stormy had started driving a cab that winter. Being an independent businesswoman was a dream come true.

"Huh!" Miss Rose remarked. It was more of a snort. "Uh, uh, uh!" And then Miss Rose herself reached over and got hold of Stormy's whiskey before it went back into the important gym bag. Miss Rose was not used to drinking tea either and she spiked hers liberally, too. She had never had tea with Spanish women before. "MMM, much better!" she said after a sip and smiled. Satisfied now, she looked around at the sky, at Stormy and at Carmen.

Carmen, who liked tea for its own sake, had drunk hers quickly. She sat on the banco in the patio in the little space between Stormy and Miss Rose and began to unravel her long black braid. "Oh you have such pretty hair!" Miss Rose, who was wearing a pink turban that day, sighed, showing all her teeth. They were very nice teeth. She put her tea down to touch the unraveling braid which felt like Grandma's spun wool. Carmen's hair was soft as angora to Miss Rose's fingers, which were callused from lighting candles with backfiring matches, shuffling tarot cards, and making tiny tiny braids from jute for her clients' made-to-order dolls. "My grand-mother had hair like yours!" Miss Rose sighed again. "Black and smooth. I'm part Cherokee, you know," she told the two women, who smiled too but did not say anything.

Instead, Stormy, feeling good from the good Cota-plus tea, leaned over and stroked Carmen's head from the top down. "Yeah," she said. "I once had long hair like that, but I cut it to spite a man who broke my heart."

"Aw, girl. Why would you do a thing like that for a man who did not deserve you in the first place?" Miss Rose asked and added, "I would not cut hair like this for anyone." She scooted right up next to Carmen still stroking the black, smooth hair. Although she could feel Miss Rose's warm tea whiskey breath next to her and Miss Rose's one good admiring insatiable eye hard on her face, Carmen looked straight ahead at the sky. She bit her bottom lip. At that hour in the winter desert it was always the same thing. Every evening Carmen was covered by the sky.

Miss Rose did not care about the sky's activities at that moment. Carmen's mouth had a bruised quality to it. Her lips, when closed, which was almost all the time, looked like she was pouting.

For a second when the sky wasn't looking or when she thought Miss Rose wasn't looking Carmen glanced sideways at la Miss Rose. Miss Rose, who never stopped talking, wasn't saying anything. The silence was almost bigger than the sky. Miss Rose reached out her bruised fingers to outline Carmen's mouth.

Stormy, who was not as impressed with Carmen's hair, started missing her own long-gone long hair and, pushing around in the gym bag, found her half pint to take a swig. Maybe the severed braid was still in her father's desk back in Truth or Consequences. She took nothing of her father's with her when she left, not even her hair. That was when she was Maruca and that was a long time ago. Miss Rose's hand stopped outlining Carmen's mouth and before Stormy realized what she was seeing Miss Rose had replaced her hand with her mouth full on Carmen's bruised-looking lips. Carmen was still looking at the sky which was straight ahead and all around them now. The moon, translucent as a fingernail, had appeared at eye level and not above as it did in other places. Then Miss Rose laughed. Stormy was shaking her head and swinging her crossed leg. "Oh Miss Rose," Stormy said with a kind of gurgly laugh, "you're too much!" Stormy was about to take another swig of whiskey when Miss Rose reached her head over and gave Stormy a kiss on the mouth, too. "Miss Rose," Stormy said afterward, putting her fingers to her mouth, "you taste good! That kiss made me hungry!"

"Oh, I bet it did, girl," Miss Rose said, "I bet it made you hungry!" And Miss Rose commenced to laughing so hard that when she threw her head back the pink turban slipped off and a tiny thing like a hummingbird or a big wasp that appeared to have been nesting inside took flight.

◁ THE RAT

Let me tell you something right now," Miss Rose said in a tone of retaliation but also, underlying it, unmitigated fear. "Miss Rose does not like rats!" She turned on the ignition and the three women started out. Miss Rose had rented a sea-blue compact.

Stormy and Carmen both kept their hastily packed bags on their laps since Miss Rose had not opened the trunk when she met them at the elevated train station exit door located under the expressway overpass. She had stayed in the car and honked. Outside it was dark and heavy black puddles along the gutters showed it had rained. Apparently there had been rats as well, or at least one rat.

Yesterday morning Stormy got a call from Miss Rose who was in Chicago on vacation. "Miss Rose! We were wondering where you were! How are you!" Stormy asked in the strained cheerful tone that she only used with la Miss Rose.

"There are two tickets waiting for you and your friend at the airport," Miss Rose announced. "When you get to the airport here, I want you two to take the train and get off at the Blue Island Avenue stop. It will only cost you a dollar and twenty-five cents each, so don't waste your money on a cab. I will be waiting for you both outside. I've got a rental, baby, so don't worry. Now, get your things together, Stormy. Don't

screw around, girl, I know how you can be. We are going to
have ourselves a nice vacation, the three of us. This is no call
from one of those men you go around with, this is me calling,
Miss Rose, so you know I do what I say. You don't have to
thank me now, darlin', just do as I tell you. You don't have
to be too smart to know that a free trip to Chicago don't come
everyday, girl." Miss Rose hung up with a sound like a little
spit knot at the end of a long threaded needle.

Miss Rose was sure full of surprises, sometimes, Stormy
told Carmen when she told her about the call."She wants to
pay *our* way to Chicago? Why? How? And I thought she didn't
know how to drive!" Carmen wondered while Stormy was
already packing.

"Listen, honey," Stormy said, pushing Carmen toward the
door so that she would go home for her things and not blow
the free trip. "Don't look a gift horse in the mouth is what
my grandmother always used to say!"

"Did your grandmother's clichés always pacify your curiosity?" Carmen asked. She put her foot in the doorway so that
Stormy could not close the door in her face.

"Cliché or not, we're getting a free trip the hell out of here
and that's all that *I* care about!"

Chicago from the air was big, big with lots of very tall
buildings. Stormy had never seen such tall buildings. Large
splats of rain hit the windshield but Miss Rose did not put
on the wipers. Miss Rose drove with her head way forward,
both hands on the steering wheel. "Miss Rose . . .," Stormy
uttered, after a few minutes of riding in silence in Miss Rose's
rented sea-blue compact. "Would you like me to drive?"
Stormy asked in a whisper. Miss Rose did not answer. She
was humming something by Aretha Franklin.

Carmen, who sat in the back, put her bag on the seat next
to her. Carmen did not know how to drive. She wished she

did but she did not. "Miss Rose," she asked, "were you born in Chicago?"

"I grew up here, baby!" Miss Rose replied. She always talked to Carmen as if Carmen *were* her baby, a beautiful, womanly Spanish baby. "Miss Rose went to school here on the South Side! Tomorrow I will take you by there! I got my diploma as a *cosmotician*, you know. I was very good, too! I got my license and everything. I most certainly did! Tomorrow Miss Rose will show you all the places where she used to hang out at when she was a girl!"

Carmen did not reply. While she knew that a cosmologist was something of a philosopher and that a cosmetologist did hair, she had never heard of a cosmotician, licensed or not.

In the front seat, next to Miss Rose, Stormy continued to clutch her gym bag and kept her eyes on Miss Rose. Carmen turned to look out of her rain-blotched window so as not to think of Miss Rose's driving or her youth which Carmen had not asked about. Carmen herself was raised all over but she was born in Texas. She never told anyone she was born in Texas. She had an accent. People did not think that Americans should have Spanish accents or, like Miss Rose, they did not think that someone who spoke Spanish was anything but Spanish, even people born in Texas.

Like Miss Rose, Carmen did not like to say where she was born either, but maybe for different reasons. "Miss Rose," Carmen wondered aloud, "does being born in a certain place mean that you won't get to where you want to go?"

"What did you say, baby?" Miss Rose called over her shoulder, her nose as close to the windshield as was possible.

Carmen looked at all the gray around them striated by rain and night, the gray of the asphalt, concrete, brick everywhere, and already she longed for the desert. There were rats in the desert, too. They lived inside saguaro cactus plants, along with spiders and owls, reptiles, and all manner of animals—a desert community. "Miss Rose," she said, "did you see a rat back there?"

"Oh, darling, do not mention that huge rat that came *scarying* right out of the sewer and ran right under my car as I was standing next to it waiting for you two! It was the biggest, most heinous thing Miss Rose could ever imagine— worse, because she did not imagine it! Oh Lord! Lord! Miss Rose saw it with her own eyes! Everytime I think of it, I wonder how I did not faint! You see what Miss Rose goes through for you?" Miss Rose shuddered at the thought of the huge heinous rat she had survived. "Lord, Lord," she added.

"Yes, Miss Rose," Stormy said quietly who had not taken her gaze off Miss Rose since she got in the car. Carmen in back closed her eyes. Just before she fell asleep she heard Stormy, using a tone that sounded like that of a hostage trying to warm up to her captor, "So, Miss Rose, what's the plan . . .?"

◁ THREE ROOMS IN THE BARRIO AND A DAHOMEY

Most people took hotel rooms on vacation, Stormy had complained to Carmen the next day when la Miss Rose announced that she had rented an apartment. They had stayed that first night in Miss Rose's motel room way on the south side of the city and far away from anything.

The apartment she rented, however, was smack in the middle of a barrio in the middle of the city. There were only three rooms in the little flat but two of them were bedrooms. The other was a kitchen; it was the first room Carmen saw when they entered. What was once a pantry had been converted into a very small bathroom. "In those days," Miss Rose said that the landlady had told her that morning when she decided to rent it, "the toilet was shared down the hall by all the tenants."

It was an old house, not nineteenth century but definitely pre–World War II. Outside in the gangway, they had seen the oldest, ugliest cat in the world. It looked a lot like a cheap old shag rug that moved. It lived in the basement and fed on rats, thereby keeping the building clean and safe. Miss Rose was content with that and said that, speaking for herself, despite the cat's unlovable appearance she would show it all the care a cat could want.

The interior walls were paint-chipped and cracked. The bedrooms were covered with high-gloss paint; one was yellow and one was blue. The kitchen was green. "Green! My favorite color!" said la Miss Rose. "Green means good luck. It means four-leaf clovers and that we never have to worry about money. It means we'll always have greener days!"

"It reminds me of guacamole, Miss Rose," Stormy said, taking her gym bag to the yellow bedroom.

"Girl, do you *ever* stop thinking about food?"

"Yes, but then, you don't want me to tell you what I think about, do you?"

"Oh please, don't. Spare Miss Rose, honey. She can guess!"

Carmen had said nothing. She pulled up a kitchen chair and sat by the window. She had an aunt who lived in Chicago. Maybe if things didn't work out here with la Miss Rose and Stormy she would look up her aunt. After all, how much worse could it be if she dropped in on a relative whom she had not seen since she was barely out of diapers?

"Family should stick together," Miss Rose said to the air, and Carmen, acting like she didn't hear what Miss Rose had just said, bent down to tie her cross-trainers.

"When Miss Rose's people were sold into slavery, sent off to face untold cruelty and isolation from their homeland, all the many people that were put on those daimons' ships became one: the Ibos, Congos, Dahomeans, Senegalese, Haoussars, Caplaous, Mandinges, Mondongues . . ."

"Mondongo? Did you say 'mondongo,' Miss Rose?" Stormy called out from the bedroom where she was lying on the bare bed that came with the furnished apartment. "I had that last night, Miss Rose! I know what that is—it's Puerto Rican stew! Right? Am I right?"

Miss Rose rolled her good eye. Her bad eye was covered up with a new patch.

"Actually I didn't have it," Stormy confessed, "but I saw it on the menu and my date told me what it is."

"How a woman could blow into town and get a date the same night is beyond me!" Miss Rose sighed. "Miss Rose has tried to tell you time and again, Stormy. You better watch out for those dollar-bill-flashin' men you like! And heaven only knows, they are no better than the ones you give your heart to, which all too often haven't had a dime to spend on you!" Miss Rose waited for a response and when none came she continued with her education of Carmen. "There were the Angolese, Libyans, Ethiopians . . ."

"Miss Rose, I never heard that the Libyans or the Ethiopians were sold into slavery into the New World."

"Neither have I," Miss Rose replied. "But I was interrupted by Miss Thing in there and lost my train of thought. Let me see. Oh yes, Miss Rose remembers her point now. These are all *my* people who have contributed to the great wisdom of the heavens that Miss Rose who was born with the veil brought with her to this life. But those of my people who *were* sold into slavery, the Dahomeans, Yorubas, Congos, Senegalese, and Sudanese, fused their tribal beliefs, forming a huge family, and thereby were able to survive despite every kind of unthinkable punishment they experienced under the tyranny of the master."

"Miss Rose, that's fantastic! I love the way you talk sometimes!" Stormy's disembodied voice continued to interrupt la Miss Rose.

"Well, that's good! Because Miss Rose loves to talk! And believe me, Miss Rose is not here in vain. No, darling. I could think of finer ways to take a vacation than doing this! But Miss Rose has a lot of work to do in this town, beginning with you two. And Carmen darling, you have got to wake up, baby. Somebody put you to sleep a long time ago and it is about time you open your eyes and smell the roses! Smell the roses! Why do you think I gave myself that beautiful name, Miss Rose? Because it ain't so much what people call you but what you call yourself, remember that, baby. There is nothing more natural and perfect that nature has given to this world than the rose!"

"Miss Rose, you talk like a poet!" Stormy called.

"May I be frank?" Carmen asked Miss Rose. Miss Rose did not nod or shake her head, but she stopped her ongoing movement about the room, since she talked and did things at the same time. She looked at Carmen as if she were surprised that Carmen had been listening at all. "I think comparing yourself to a rose is straight out of nineteenth-century male romanticism . . ."

"Oh there ain't nothing straight about Miss Rose," she laughed before Carmen could finish being frank. "But Miss Rose doesn't have any more time now. Tonight is my high school reunion and I have been nominated for the Dick Clark Award! So I am on my way downtown to Marshall Field to get myself something to wear! Adios, my muchachas bonitas!"

Miss Rose grabbed her handbag and went out the door. Carmen and Stormy listened to the click-click of Miss Rose's high-heeled boots and then the slam of the outside door at the foot of the stairs. "What is a Dick Clark Award?" Carmen wondered aloud.

"Forever young, honey, it means that la Miss Rose will be forever young! Bless her crazy loca heart! All I know is I've never met a negra like her!"

"I've never met anyone like her either," Carmen said in a low, lethargic voice. As she spoke, she leaned her head against the open windowsill. In the distance there was the "Yankee Doodle" melody of an ice-cream truck and the air was filled with the smell of the city summer in bloom, Mexican food frying and a crying infant downstairs, a loud boom box playing Vicente Fernández's rendition of "Amor Eterno." Teenage boys on the corner were screaming at each other, "Oye, cabrón! Where the hell have you been?"

Stormy got up and, putting a hand on Carmen's shoulder, she asked softly, "Carmen, honey, why are you crying?"

◁ Doctor Rose

I have an aunt in Chicago," Carmen announced one afternoon to Miss Rose.

It was another very clear but very hot day. The sky was blue but small because it was in the city. Although it was as hot as the desert the city air smelled of exhaust fumes and something close to chorizo. Maybe it was chorizo, Carmen thought, sticking her head out of the window for a moment to sniff her downstairs neighbor's lunch. It was hard to tell.

Too many memories stirred up in the last few weeks by such things like the heavy odor of frying chorizo, the sounds of Mexican mothers calling for their children, and sudden loud *loud* music from cars cruising around the block playing

"El día que me quieras" and other achingly sad songs had Carmen more quiet and more melancholy than ever.

Memories unleashed, Carmen was now all but paralyzed with childhood recollections too painful to have ever let out on her own. She sat very still, taking it all in and letting nothing out.

Carmen and Miss Rose had gone to the store earlier and purchased an oscillating fan and having it on the kitchen table were both receiving the benefits of its relentless hot air.

There was still no relief from the heat.

"She is my father's sister so I haven't seen her since I was a baby. I also have family in Indiana—on my mother's side." It was rare for Carmen to talk about herself. She got Miss Rose's attention right away.

While Carmen reminisced, however reluctantly, Miss Rose was cooking something sweet-smelling. She said it was for her St. John's Eve feast, which was just around the corner. "Why don't you invite your aunt over for a visit?" Miss Rose asked. La Miss Rose pronounced "aunt" with an elegant "ah" sound. Carmen said it like "ant."

"I haven't seen her since I was a baby," Carmen said again.

"Miss Rose is not deaf, puddin'. I have talked to you about that. What Miss Rose means is that because you have not seen your auntie for so long it does not mean you can never see her again."

It may have been the heat but Carmen was feeling sadder by the minute. She did not remember her aunt much and therefore had nothing further to say of her. She did remember vividly, however, the fields of her childhood and the years of following harvest after harvest with her family. "I know onions and I know potatoes," Carmen said.

Miss Rose scratched her turban and turned back to the stove. She picked up a wooden spoon bought at the Maxwell Street

Market the previous Sunday and began to stir her pot. Miss Rose took a taste from the tip of the spoon. She thought for a second and then said, "This needs some more sugar! The spirits require lots of sugar with their black-eyed peas and rice!"

"I don't know sugarcanes but I know chiles," Carmen continued. "Red, green, wide and flat, small and plump. Thousands of them all around you. I can tell a hot pepper from a mild one just from sight, without even smelling it."

Miss Rose began fussing loudly with her pot of congris doing everything possible to show that she was finding Carmen's rare attempt at conversation difficult to appreciate.

"I know fruits too, Miss Rose," Carmen said. "Pears, apples, watermelons. But berries and grapes, they're the worst."

Miss Rose turned to look at Carmen with the wooden spoon in her hand which suddenly appeared menacing in her grip. La Miss Rose liked food very much. For a moment she did not understand what appeared to be Carmen's aversion to produce. "Is the smell of Miss Rose's congris upsetting you, baby?"

"Once you've spent a season picking thorny cranberries or reaching as high as you can with your tiny child body to cherry trees or pricking your fingers to shreds filling bushels with blackberries, you lose your taste for pie, Miss Rose," Carmen said. Miss Rose studied Carmen.

After a long minute, Miss Rose said, "Miss Rose knows one thing you cannot say you've lost your taste for, and that is her specially prepared Island rum!" She ran into her room. Coming back out with a bottle she quickly poured three glasses full. Miss Rose placed one before Carmen and the other was set aside for someone she called "Grandma" but who wasn't there. She drank hers right away.

"Now, I would not share my rum with Stormy who does

not need this kind of medicine—since any kind of medicine when you take too much of it can have the reverse effect on you! But Miss Rose can wait. Sooner or later she'll come around; they all do!"

Carmen took a sip of Miss Rose's homemade Island rum. Miss Rose looked pleased.

"Anyway, honey cakes, you go ahead. Have yourself a little of Miss Rose's good medicine today. St. John's Eve is coming around soon and Miss Rose is going to bring you back to the living; you just wait and see."

Miss Rose leaned over near Carmen's face. She put a finger under one of Carmen's eyes and pulled down the skin. She did the same to the other, examining the whites of both eyes. "Baby, you're lucky Miss Rose got here when she did, too! Now have a glass of Miss Rose's medicine and forget about all those years of working in the sun. My people picked cotton and watermelon just like yours. And they picked sugar beets and potatoes just like yours, darlin'. You got all those generations of broken backs and broken spirits in your blood and more than memory, you still got them damn calluses on your hands and feet! Miss Rose saw them the first time you came to see her! You got a bigger question than the one you asked that day! Why are you going to pay good money to Miss Rose to see why someone who is probably not worth your tears and time to begin with is not talking to you? No, girlfriend, you have a bigger question to ask, but for now, you have got to learn to laugh."

◁ DAN

"Ahhhh!" Stormy shrieked suddenly and ran out the door. Carmen looked under the kitchen table where Stormy had just lifted the bright oilcloth. Underneath, in the cool shade, there was a large glass aquarium and inside it a very pale snake, with a long, quick tongue.

The door opened again. "Miss Rose," Stormy asked, sticking her head in the door and easing her body back in slowly. "Did you have to bring Dan with you?"

Miss Rose was in her room. She had put up a curtain and neither Carmen nor Stormy was allowed to enter. Her voice came through the curtain, "Yes. Did you expect me to leave him in the car indefinitely?"

"You mean Dan has been in the car the whole time, since we came to Chicago?"

"Well, Miss Rose could not very well leave her most sacred possession behind now, could she?"

"What do you feed it?" Carmen asked. She had a pot of frijoles on the stove. Obviously she was not thinking of feeding the snake beans, although beans were all she really knew how to cook. Since she was very young, whenever she was tried by life Carmen responded by making beans. Consequently she made very good beans. "It's the pork fat," she told people. Even though as a vegetarian she did not like to think about pork fat, it was still the secret to good beans.

There was a pause and then Miss Rose said, "Newborn rodents."

"Oh, yech, Miss Rose! I thought you didn't like rats! Where do you get such nasty things to feed it?"

"La chatte," Miss Rose answered. She and the oldest, ugliest cat in the world were now on very good terms. This explained Miss Rose's frequent trips to the basement despite her fear of rats.

"Miss Rose," Stormy asked, "did you also bring Maïtresse Venus?"

"Of course Miss Rose brought along Maïtresse Venus! Do you think Dan would come without her?" This time Miss

Rose volunteered the answer before Stormy had to ask. Maïtresse Venus is in the bathroom, darling. Underneath the basin."

Another snake, more mice, three rooms, Mexican beans cooking all day on the stove, people always complaining. Carmen sighed. It was beginning to feel more and more like her childhood. And although she was very far away from the desert, most of the day in her mind that is where she went.

"Well, at least Venus feeds on bananas!" Stormy told Carmen.

Miss Rose peeked out from behind her curtain door. "What else would a goddess prefer, but sweet, long, soft plaintains all day long!"

"Well, *I* could think of something," Stormy said, smiling.

"Yes, darling, but Miss Rose would rather not hear it."

Carmen didn't mind the snake or snakes, which did not scare her. She *did* find, however, the framed picture of the president that Miss Rose had nailed over the front door scary. Miss Rose, who did not like to explain things, nevertheless did reply to Carmen's inquiry. It seemed that in *her* tradition, the origins of which Carmen still had not been able to put her finger on, kings were appointed by God or the gods. Although the president was not a king but ostensibly held office as result of popular vote, it did not hurt a person such as herself to have the protection of one's principal government leader and to therefore pay him respect.

"A person such as yourself?" Carmen asked.

"Yes, sweet cakes, Miss Rose has many great powers and great gifts. Unfortunately, however, they are not always appreciated by the local authorities."

◁ HAPPINESS WONG CHINESE ANCESTOR

"Did Miss Rose ever tell you ladies about her Chinese ancestor?" Miss Rose was standing by the kitchen window with Dan around her shoulders.

"No, but I *do* remember you mentioning your Irish ancestors!" Stormy said. She still did not like Dan and kept her distance. Because she spent so much time at the mirror in the bathroom, however, she ignored the snake that lived beneath the basin, even when she heard the occasional tiny snap of a water bug the snake caught between its slender jaws.

"That's true, that's true!" Miss Rose said. "And that is why Miss Rose is so lucky! I've got the luck of the Irish! But I also had a Chinese ancestor. He worked on the railroad in California."

"You had a Chinese ancestor?" Carmen asked.

"Carmen, doll, you must stop repeating everything Miss Rose says. You are giving her the distinct impression that either you do not believe Miss Rose or you are not a very bright individual. And Miss Rose would not like to think that either of those two conclusions could be true." Miss Rose began to move snake-like with her snake. She was preparing for St. John's Eve, she told them.

Neither Stormy nor Carmen had ever heard of St. John's Eve. "If Miss Rose tells you she had a Chinese ancestor you do not have to repeat it. Believe me, sweetness, *I* heard what Miss Rose said!"

"Miss Rose, instead of repeating yourself so many times why don't you finish telling us about your Chinese great-grandfather or whatever you say he was?" Stormy called from the bathroom. She painted a black line over each eyelid that ended at the corner in a tiny black wing. Then, very, very carefully, Stormy outlined her lips with a dark dark pencil.

Finally came the pièce de résistance: her fire red lip gloss. Formerly the pièce de résistance had been a phony black Marilyn Monroe mole that she stuck just above the lip, but she had lost it in her date's car the night before.

Stormy came out of the bathroom, her face done, rollers in her hair and began to pull them off. "I've been thinking, what do you think I'd look like as a blond?"

"I would not let you go home to your mother," Miss Rose replied.

"I just don't think it would look natural on you," Carmen answered.

"You mean I'm too dark, don't you?" Stormy laughed a little cynical laugh. "Hell, I don't care about that."

"I suspect that there are many things you do not concern yourself with, dumpling," Miss Rose said. "One of them is the conversation Miss Rose was trying to have, if you don't mind. It was about my Chinese ancestor."

"You had a Chinese ancestor?" Carmen repeated.

"Girl! What did I just tell you! If you do not wake up soon Miss Rose is going to have to put some very drastic measures into effect. You are going to be here on St. John's Eve, aren't you, baby? Because Miss Rose is going to be especially dancing for you!"

Stormy peeked out the window. A second later there was a whistle. "Girl! Would you please come away from that window? Didn't your mother raise you right at all? How can you be looking out half naked?" Miss Rose, herself in a silk kimono, was leaning halfway out the adjacent window with Dan. It was a very humid evening.

Stormy went to her room to dress and called to Miss Rose to please say whatever the hell it was she had to say about her so-called Chinese ancestor and get it over with. Even though Stormy still reserved a certain respect for Miss Rose that she did not save for anyone else it was beginning to wear thin as the weeks wore on. Carmen had asked Stormy why it was that she treated Miss Rose with respect while Stormy would not hold her tongue for anyone else. "That ain't respect!" Stormy said. "That's fear! I'm afraid of la Miss Rose!"

"Why?" Carmen asked, scratching her cheek. She always scratched her cheek when she was puzzled. Carmen did not find Miss Rose frightening. She had come to no conclusions about Miss Rose at all. The only thing that Carmen ever wondered about concerning Miss Rose was how she had found herself one day in Chicago living in the same flat with the woman.

"When I first met Miss Rose, I went to her because I was really in love with this guy, right? He was this white dude with a lot of money that I met at the club that I was working at. You know, when I used to dance. But even though I was all right to party with, he didn't want anything else to do with me. So I heard about la Miss Rose and went to her. You won't believe the crazy things that woman had me doing trying to get that dude to fall in love with me!"

"Like the powders?"

"Like crazy things, mujer! Take my word for it!"

"Like what?" Carmen asked again.

"Things that required bodily fluids, okay?"

"Like blood?"

"Yeah! Like blood—my moon blood! We didn't kill no animals if that's what you're thinking!"

"Well, so, did it work?"

"Hell yeah it worked!"

Carmen was surprised. She had only had a question when she went to Miss Rose and even that much Miss Rose had not ever answered.

"I bet you don't even have a Chinese ancestor, Miss Rose!" Stormy now teased.

"Miss Rose does too have a Chinese ancestor. As soon as someone you believe in dies they become your ancestor. His name was Happiness Wong, my Chinese ancestor from California. He taught Miss Rose all kinds of wonderful things when she was a little sweet girl. Miss Rose was not Miss Rose then but a sweet little innocent child who still nevertheless knew a lot because she was born with the veil as I've said. He said that if you eat well, not a lot, just what you need, keep away from red meat, do plenty of exercise—my great-grandfather could do that stuff—you know! What do you call it?" She began flapping her arms slowly like a crane.

"What, Miss Rose? Fly?" Stormy asked, clearly impatient now.

"Tai chi, Miss Rose," said Carmen, who was beginning to decipher *how* Miss Rose thought, although not why she thought what she did. She looked at Stormy, who was dressed to the nines in a purple sequined dress. Stormy shook her head just enough for Carmen to notice as she put on a pair of rhinestone earrings.

"Yeah! Yeah! That's it, baby, tai chi! He did that every morning. Eat good, exercise, early to bed and early to rise and you could easily live to be one hundred years old. And you know it worked for him because he was about that age when I was a child."

"I bet you read that on some cereal box!" Stormy said. She picked up her purse and went for the door.

"Miss Rose may not remember all the Chinese wisdom her great ancestor Happiness Wong tried to impart upon her so long ago, Stormy, but you better be careful, girl! Them streets out there are not safe. It ain't like you were back home in that desert town you've been used to, where there are two people and an old crow hanging off the bar stools all night. There are more men sneaking about in the shadows here than there are spiders back in your backyard. Miss Rose can't go out and bail you out of jail every night, either. So be careful, Stormy, girl . . ."

Miss Rose went on like that although Stormy had gone out the door with her last remark to Miss Rose. Miss Rose hurried with Dan out to the fire escape. When she spotted Stormy down in the gangway heading for the street, Miss Rose, ignoring the whistles below, began to shout, "Stormy! Stormy! You be careful with Miss Rose's rental, baby! Miss Rose has to turn it in tomorrow morning!"

◁ THE SCIENCE OF ODORS

"Oh man! This tonto is coming to pick me up in five minutes and I'm still not ready!" Stormy always referred to her dates as tontos. From the brief experiences Carmen had had with Stormy's dates, she did not find Stormy's assessment of her male companions too harsh. Rushing out of the bathroom Stormy asked Carmen, "Do you have any perfume? I just ran out!" Before Carmen could answer Stormy went into the forbidden headquarters of Miss Rose. La Miss Rose was not at home at the time.

"Oh here's some!" Stormy said and came out of Miss Rose's room sniffing a milk gallon filled with something aromatic Miss Rose had put together herself. There were some leafy twigs floating inside. Stormy poured some in one hand and sprinkled it on her face and chest. She dabbed a little behind each ear.

Ready now, Stormy smiled at Carmen who as usual was sitting on a kitchen chair by the window reading. One day, Stormy hoped, her friend Carmen would snap to it. She should have some fun. Although Carmen *was* a few years older than herself, she wasn't *that* old yet. Carmen reminded Stormy a lot of her own suffering mother, may she rest in peace. Stormy didn't have much time for suffering women. But there was still hope for Carmen. It was not too late for her as it was for Stormy's mother who died of unhappiness. "Carmen, hon', you can't spend your life locked up in your room reading and writing all the time! Who do you think you are anyway—what's her name, the nun poet?" After a moment, she added with a little laugh, "Come to think of it, you *do* remind me a little of Sor . . ." Then Stormy's eyes disappeared in her head. With a little "Oh," she hit the floor.

Carmen said "Oh!" too, and dropping her book hurried over to Stormy. Stormy's face had gone pale. When Carmen took her in her arms and shook her Stormy did not respond.

Miss Rose came in just then. She had been out passing out flyers to drum up some business. "OH!" Miss Rose gasped, immediately taking in the gravity of the situation. But when she saw the spilled gallon on the floor next to Stormy she dropped to her knees. Her cotton skirt crumpled around her like a big, white lily. Feeling Stormy's pulse Miss Rose began to chant: "Our Father, Hail Mary, Creed, Glory be to the Father, Hail Mary, hear my prayers, Holy Angels, we are on our knees at the feet of Mary, Saint Rose, hear us, Jesus, hear us, Saint Peter, give us the key which opens the gate, Saint Anthony hear us!" It was a very long prayer. She took a breath and continued: "The angel of the Lord said to Mary that she was pregnant with Jesus Christ, Saint Philomena, virgin and martyr . . . Holy virgins, hear us, Alas, alas, Mary Magdalene!" Miss Rose opened her good eye and for a second glared at Stormy. Then she went on: "Oh, Lord Jesus in the Host, grace, Mary, grace! We hail Thee, O Mary, hear our prayers and place us in heaven to serve you! Great God intercede for us, Saint

Joseph intercede with Jesus for us, Faith, Hope, and Charity hear us! All martyrs and saints hear us, Saint Philip, hear us, Saint John the Baptist, your servant is here . . .!" Stormy's eyes had remained open but her pupils were lost so that only the whites showed. Her body was limp all over. Miss Rose went on praying. This time she was hailing what she called her *houn'gans* and *loas*. Carmen wasn't sure if they were saints or spirits, but she began to repeat after la Miss Rose just the same. "Hail Danbhalah and Aida Wédo!" Miss Rose shouted and Carmen echoed, "Hail Danbhalah and Aida Wédo!" At which point Venus crawled, rather quickly for a snake, out of the bathroom toward Stormy. Dan was also working his way out of his tank.

"Ogou Chango!" Miss Rose called next. Carmen looked at Dan and then at Venus, both heading in their direction. Not knowing what might come around next if she kept reinforcing Miss Rose's chants, she stayed quiet.

"Toutou Mambo, Toutou Houn'gan, Congo, Nago, Zo!" Miss Rose said.

She stopped hailing.

Dan and Venus met and entwined on Stormy's motionless stomach. Miss Rose sighed. Then, leaning over, she said in a very personal way, "Stormy, come to the living, girl . . ." Stormy, first with a few blinks, then with a tiny groan, did just that.

◁ THE SIGN

"There's a sign nailed outside the front door, Miss Rose," Stormy said, returning from her daily meeting. Every week it was a different recovery program for Stormy since her near-death experience with Miss Rose's potent homemade perfume. She looked a little tipsy. Sometimes after meetings, the group went out for a drink, overwrought not so much from telling their own stories but from hearing all the others.

"A sign?" Carmen asked. Today Carmen was ironing, putting plenty of starch in Miss Rose's white cotton skirts and blouses. When Miss Rose wasn't looking plenty of starch went in Miss Rose's one-piece bloomers, too. Miss Rose called them "Mother Hubbards" and stitched her cotton underwear herself. Stiff Mother Hubbards should give Miss Rose a laugh, Carmen thought.

"I am very aware of the sign, my deleece," Miss Rose said cheerfully. The sight of Carmen ironing her wash was heavenly.

"Yeah," Stormy said to Carmen. "It says 'Société La Fleur Cé Nous.'" Stormy pronounced it with a Spanish accent. Miss Rose smiled broadly. "Good! Miss Rose *knew* Spanish people wouldn't have any trouble reading French!" Sometimes Miss Rose amazed even herself at how well she knew people.

"What does it mean?" Stormy asked.

"It means 'We are the Flower Society,' of course!"

"No, what does it *mean*, Miss Rose?"

"It *means* that anybody can come to Miss Rose anytime for healing and divination and for anything else their hearts desire. Miss Rose has just updated her price list for her services." She pointed to a yellow notepad across the room. Carmen stopped ironing to take a look at the list. Miss Rose's supposed services were very intriguing.

"Hey, Stormy," Carmen said, a little amused, "here's one for you! 'How to Stay on the Job': you bring a handful of pecans to Miss Rose and both of you eat them. Later you throw the hulls in a place where nothing will move them and you stay unmoved, too! Worth a try, don't you think?"

Stormy ignored Carmen, who she thought was being sarcastic.

"Although you have grossly summarized the full extent of that service, I recognize it as my New Orleans recipe," Miss Rose said proudly. At the top of her list was a disclaimer: "All services are for Entertainment Only. All Goods are Sold as Novelties." In fine print at the bottom of her list, however, Miss Rose stated that while her work was not guaranteed she had had good results so far. "Pecans ain't all that special here," she told the women. "Maybe seedless grapes might work."

"No grapes unless they're organically grown," Carmen interjected instantly, wondering right afterward what Miss Rose might propose the client plant after eating a seedless grape.

Carmen, who continued to read Miss Rose's list, said, "Of course, getting rid of bad luck should come first. It says here, two pounds of birdseed, two pounds of sugar . . ." But noting that Stormy was acting very annoyed with her suggestions Carmen stopped short, put the list down, and went back to her ironing.

Stormy promptly picked it up. In addition to Miss Rose's services there was also a list of goods for various needs. Powders ranged from "Trouble with your Landlord" to "Follow-Me." They were very reasonably priced.

Miss Rose turned to Stormy. "And you of all people should know Miss Rose can do what she says. Don't come here looking at Miss Rose like she doesn't!"

"Yeah? Like making a man fall in love with you and act like a jerk with you—a bigger jerk than before?" Stormy asked.

"I only promised he'd fall in love with you, darling. Miss Rose is not accountable for bad taste."

◁ Can a White Man Really Love a Woman Who Is Not White Without Being Mojoed?

"Well, of course he can, sugar!" Miss Rose said to Stormy, who asked because she had been in love a long time with the only man on earth that she could not have just by snapping her fingers and could not figure out why. "What no man can do and what no woman can do is love someone until they love themselves!" Miss Rose added in her I-am-trying-not-to-be-patronizing-only-wise tone. Stormy still seemed unappreciative of the advice but said nothing.

The three women were on their way to the lake. It was St. John's Eve, the summer solstice to most people. But for Miss Rose it was the most important date of the year. Observing St. John on his day, there was nothing you couldn't ask of him, she kept telling Carmen and Stormy. It was a very secretive rite, she added, making sure they knew how lucky they were to be part of the Flower Society that year.

Anyone who tried to sneak a peek at them while performing the secret rites by the lake would go blind, she said. And anyone telling people about what they did on St. John's Eve would wake up with her tongue withered, she warned.

Stormy and Carmen nodded and did all that Miss Rose instructed. Of course, they knew they had the option to refuse but, just as St. John's head was placed before Salome, who can refuse power on a silver platter?

"A bird in the hand is worth two in the bush, as my grandmother used to say," Stormy whispered to Carmen later when Carmen asked what she thought of la Miss Rose's St. John's Eve.

"What does that have to do with anything?" Carmen asked in her patient although often skeptical tone.

"Nothing," Stormy said, "but come to think of it, my grandmother really knew her English, don't you think? I mean, she was always talking that way and she always quoted those sayings right. They're not easy to get straight, you know."

"I know," Carmen agreed.

"Although I don't think she always knew what they meant," Stormy admitted.

"I know," Carmen said. Stormy was right. English was like a tough wire that could only be straight if you had had it from the very beginning. If you started out in life speaking anything else, no matter how hard you tried, you would spend the rest of your life trying to straighten out that wire. And still, no matter what, it would always be a little bent.

The moon the night of St. John's Eve, as the three women walked across Grant Park toward the lake, was not full but it was very high, above the tallest trees, higher than the skyscrapers. It looked like a Chinese paper lantern. Stormy was carrying the pot of congris. Carmen was charged with two large shopping bags. They were both almost too heavy to carry. Miss Rose brought along an exquisitely carved baby coffin in which Dan was being transported for the ceremonies.

"When Miss Rose was a young girl in Chicago," Miss Rose said as they got off the bus and began their trek toward the lakefront, "her big sister took her to hear Malcolm X speak! Mmmm-mm! Now *that* man was fine! That red-haired rascal! *His* color was natural, you know."

Stormy patted her own hair which she had just had cut and dyed. Despite her two friends' low opinion of her new style, Stormy was enjoying being a blond, although it had turned out more orange than yellow.

"What you two don't understand," she told Carmen and Miss Rose when they first saw her, "is that *my* generation isn't hung up on things like that. You can be black and go platinum blond and it don't mean you don't like being black.

And you can be a man wearing earrings on both ears and hair down to there and not be into men! It's a diversity statement. That's all!"

Both women stared at Stormy without comment. Then she added, "It don't mean I don't think there still are racists out there! And I don't think dying my hair blond is going to change how they act toward me or feel about me, either."

Although it was true that Stormy had dyed her hair only out of boredom, she was convinced that the rich white playboy she was in love with had not taken her seriously because she was a Mexican. Mexican, poor, and once a stripper.

Nevertheless they were drawn to each other from the beginning. They got high together. They partied all night. Then he'd go home to his wife.

Until Miss Rose mojoed him. Then he left his wife. Then he wouldn't let Stormy alone.

The other night at a club, Stormy thought she had seen him.

She was still in love with him.

"Malcolm X was fine all right and a powerful speaker and he did leave an impression on me," Miss Rose said. "But when I was a young woman just out of *cosmotology* school my ideal man would have been a combination of Miles Davis and Fidel Castro! I once saw Miles Davis perform, too! Do you know he played the whole time with his back to the audience?" Miss Rose laughed. "Yeah! Miles didn't care about what people thought of him. He just played on and on. Miss Rose still remembers that night."

◁ **HEAVEN FOR A SMALL FEE**

The day came when Carmen finally decided she would look up her long-lost aunt. After that, she'd go home. Actually, the aunt had never been lost. Carmen had just lost touch.

"What's wrong, baby?" Miss Rose asked when Carmen told her about her plans to leave. "Are you mad at Miss Rose about something? She has already said she was very sorry about how St. John's Eve turned out!"

"Miss Rose, I've told you that I don't blame you about our getting arrested. We didn't know that the beach was closed when we went swimming!"

That was not the only reason why the three women, all slightly inebriated at the time, were hauled off to jail for the night. Carmen and Stormy, following Miss Rose's lead, had drunk Island rum, ate congris, and fed some to the spirits in the water. La Société la Fleur Cé Nous started a bonfire, kicked up sand, chanting and dancing in their Mother Hubbards, and finally stripped down and went bathing in the cold lake. That was when the police turned up.

Miss Rose gave a long, loud, sad sigh.

Her healing and divination practice was in full swing. Many of Miss Rose's endless flow of new clients were Spanish-speaking. She made herself understood by speaking in a funny kind of French. Many of her clients were English-speaking, too. Men in suits and ties came from City Hall during their lunch hour. Some men without jobs or whose wives they thought did not love them anymore also came to see Miss Rose. But most of Miss Rose's clients were women, all kinds of women. There was a particular demand for Miss Rose's oils—Van Van Oil, Secret Lavender, and many more which Carmen, acting as Miss Rose's assistant on occasion, learned to prepare. She liked Miss Rose's oils best, too.

The powders were always a popular item.

Stormy was hardly ever around anymore. She was now writing poetry, taking a yoga class, and had started driving a cab. She was also in love. Although Carmen had not found the news in her friend's love life particularly surprising, Stormy for a change was playing her hand close to her chest. The usual demands she made on her other men were not evident this time. He gave her no costly gifts. He was not wining and dining her every night. Stranger still, Stormy never referred to him as a tonto.

After Carmen told Miss Rose about her plans, Miss Rose went into her room to meditate. At least Carmen thought Miss Rose was meditating when after a few minutes heavy incense smoke rolled out from underneath the curtain. Following the incense, however, came the alternate sounds of chimes and rattles and then the steady beat of a little drum. At one point, Carmen thought she heard Miss Rose sob.

Maybe it was the water drum.

Finally Miss Rose came back out. She was smiling. She looked refreshed and as if it were her idea she said, "Carmen, baby, Miss Rose thinks it would be a big mistake if you did not try to find your aunt before you left Chicago."

Carmen nodded and went to the phonebook. There seemed to be about seven hundred listings with Carmen's last name. She eliminated all the listings with first names that as far as she knew could not be remotely connected to her aunt.

That left her with about three hundred.

"Miss Rose, can't *you* find my aunt for me?"

Miss Rose was shaking her head. She pushed the curtain aside for Carmen to enter her consultation room. "You know I could find a needle in a haystack if I had to! Miss Rose has helped the depressed, oppressed, and those just in a mess, why couldn't she help you, baby? Fortunately, Miss Rose's visibility level is very clear today. You know what the fee for finding folks is, just leave it right there for St. Peter, baby. St. Peter, St. Peter, open the gate!" Miss Rose called out to the summer day, and then added, "I thought this girl would never come around!"

◁ COME-TO-ME (IN POWDER OR OIL) . . . $7.00/OZ.

Although Miss Rose did not require Carmen to use any bodily fluids in their work to find Carmen's aunt, there was all manner of burning candles and sweet-scented baths that Carmen took for weeks. At one point a small pigeon was involved.

While Carmen waited for her aunt's reappearance in her life, she and Miss Rose planned Stormy's wedding. "Oh, my, my!" Miss Rose said when Stormy tried on the lace-mini dress that Miss Rose had just altered. "You remind me of my bride at my wedding!" she said and pulling the patch away momentarily, dabbed her bad eye and then the good one. Adding for Carmen's benefit, "You remember, honey cone, I told you about that young Spanish girl and me, how she left me high and dry after all I did for her?"

Carmen nodded.

Miss Rose cheered up and admired Stormy in her wedding dress. "You remind me of me too, honey. For my wedding I made both of our dresses! You remember, don't you? That's right! You were the one in charge of the video! Whatever happened to that video of my wedding anyway? Didn't I pay you good money for that?"

Stormy twirled around in her mini–wedding dress and giggled. She was a pretty bride-to-be. "I gave you a copy, remember, Miss Rose! Look around in all that junk you got in there." Stormy pointed to Miss Rose's room. "I bet you'll find it!"

Miss Rose crossed her arms. She looked at Carmen, who was holding the pincushion for her. "Would *you* like to see the video of Miss Rose's wedding, darlin'?" Miss Rose asked Carmen. Without waiting for an answer, she added, "No, no, never mind! I would just end up crying! Miss Rose can't take weddings! They always make her cry!"

"Are you going to cry at my wedding, too, Miss Rose?" Stormy asked. Without a mother to attend her wedding, Stormy thought that Miss Rose crying at her wedding would be nice.

"Oh, yes, Stormy, baby! Miss Rose is especially going to cry at your wedding! She is going to throw rose petals and rice at you and your playboy-turned-po'boy groom who followed you from hell and wish you both lots of beautiful healthy babies! But most of all she is going to hope that his wife doesn't show up to spoil things for you both!"

"Miss Rose, I *told* you he got a divorce—that's why he's so broke! Don't you believe him or what?"

"Miss Rose believes in love, darlin'!" Miss Rose said, sprinkling a little rosewater on her neck. "Miss Rose believes in love," she said again. "And fortunately for you, baby, he has plenty of it for you! Thank the spirits and the holy saints!" Miss Rose sprinkled Stormy with her rosewater but as she turned to sprinkle Carmen, Carmen was reaching for something that had been slipped under the doorway.

"Look, Miss Rose," Stormy said, reading over Carmen's shoulder. "It ain't pizza. It's a flower sale! Let's call! I want lots and lots of flowers at my wedding party!"

Carmen put the ad on the table. "I'll call, Stormy," she said. "Getting the flowers for your wedding before I go is the least I can do."

Carmen turned to ask Miss Rose if she knew where the cellular phone was but Miss Rose was in her room shuffling and moving the many cardboard boxes she kept stored in there. "You have got to see the video of Miss Rose's wedding!" Miss Rose called loudly over her shoulder. "She had flowers. She had good champagne. None of that cheap stuff that doesn't have any bubbles, you know the kind I mean, Stormy. You're going to have to get yourself some for your Wedding Bath anyway! No expense was spared for Miss Rose's wedding day! And if you are half as in love as I was—and I know you are, girl—don't be cheap with your wedding either! Love only comes around now and then!" Then Miss Rose let out a squeal. "Here it is!"

◁ LA MISS ROSE'S WEDDING VIDEO

One of Stormy's many failed ambitions—but nevertheless a dream that kept her going—was to be a cinematographer. She never studied anywhere. She took lots of pictures all the time with an Instamatic she found in the ladies' room at the Peek-a-Boo Lounge where she had worked for eight years as a dancer. Some people really liked the fotos she took of them but some only saw them as snapshots. Her career with film began and ended with the use of Miss Rose's camcorder. Miss Rose lent it to her that very night, hiring Stormy, who was as close to a professional as anyone she knew, to videotape her wedding. Stormy really wanted to do it and she came cheap. But she could hardly have gotten any practice beforehand, not having her own camcorder, so she was not ashamed that most of what she filmed was too dark to see.

Carmen watched the video as la Miss Rose and Stormy filled in the big blanks left by Stormy's shortcomings as a videographer.

Still, Carmen caught a grayish glimpse of the five-tier cake with not a little plastic bride and groom at the top, not two brides either, but two splendid doves made of sparkling white sugar.

There were lots of people moving about, all dancing to the soulful tunes being spun by a local DJ. Mostly you could not see faces because the lighting was so bad and because that was during Stormy's days of heaviest intoxication, but occasionally a hand or smile came into view. Stormy and la Miss Rose would rewind and press "replay" over and over until one of them figured out to whom the hand or smile belonged.

"What would you like to wish the happy couple?" Stormy would ask around randomly. "Oh, I don't know," someone would say, "a long and happy life together, I guess."

And then, there were the lovers in identical white lace dresses, tightly embraced, mouths locked in French kiss while slow-dancing to "Natural Woman" by Aretha Franklin.

Miss Rose let out a long sigh and dabbed her eyes. She always did love everything by Aretha Franklin.

◁ Miss Rose's Ship

Periodically during the heat wave, Miss Rose stepped into the portable shower fully clothed, blasted herself with cold water, and went back to whatever it was she was doing.

"The stars and the heavens do not make mistakes," Miss Rose told Carmen. Carmen had ordered seven dozen roses for Stormy's reception. She insisted until the end that she had said seven. When seventy dozen showed up, the owner, who had a chain of flower shops and nurseries throughout the city and suburbs, came out of retirement and delivered them personally to take a look at her splendid new customer. The owner, of all people, turned out to be Carmen's long-lost aunt. She had ended up a very successful businesswoman.

So much had happened since Stormy's wedding. Stormy

was still on her honeymoon in the Wisconsin Dells. Miss Rose was packing. And Carmen was suddenly an heiress.

"Well, darlin', at least your auntie was happy to be reunited with her only family before she died. And she did die peacefully in her bed. Peaceful and rich. Nobody can ask for much more than that!" Miss Rose said.

Carmen was on her way to her aunt's funeral. La Miss Rose eyed Carmen. "What are you planning on doing with all that money, anyway, baby?"

Carmen shrugged her shoulders. Then she asked: "How 'bout if I buy you a little house all your own in New Orleans, Miss Rose? Where you can practice your healing and run your business?"

Miss Rose winced.

"Maybe I'll get Stormy her own cab, too, when she gets back," Carmen thought aloud. She kept thinking, and added, "Then, I guess I'll have to go and take care of all those baby trees and beautiful flowers I've inherited. What do you think, Miss Rose?"

Miss Rose put her two hands halfway up toward the sky. In a kind of chant-like tone she said: "In the name of Madame la Lune, La Belle Vénus, in the name of the woman Brillant-Soleil, Madame Magie, la Négresse Cordon Blue, Négresse l'Arc-en-Ciel, Négresse l'Océan." Miss Rose kneeled down and knocked on the ground three times. Then she said, looking up at Carmen as if she was her guardian angel incarnate, "Miss Rose thinks today is a very good day!"

◁ ¡Adios Mariquita Linda!

Stormy was driving her new black limousine. She had just taken out her chauffeur's license. She and Carmen were riding Miss Rose to the airport in style. Miss Rose sat in the back and spoke to Stormy over the intercom. "Did Miss Rose tell you ladies that her sweet girl wrote to her and said she had returned all Miss Rose's things to her old apartment?"

Carmen and Stormy exchanged glances. Carmen preferred to sit in the front with Stormy. She liked Miss Rose now, very much, but she did not like riding in the back of a limousine, even if it were owned and driven by her friend. Stormy picked up the intercom. "So does that mean you have forgiven her, Miss Rose?"

Miss Rose was laughing in the back. "Miss Rose never had anything against the girl! I told you that! My girl was just not ready, that's all!"

Stormy and Carmen looked at each other again. Stormy asked, "So, do you think she's ready now, Miss Rose?"

"She is on her way to meet me in New Orleans! I always knew she'd come back! Miss Rose knows a great many things she can't always prove right away."

They pulled up in front of the terminal and all three jumped out at once to say goodbye. The sky was heavy with leaden clouds. The heat wave was about to break.

"Adieu, my darlin's!" Miss Rose called over her shoulder. All her things, with the exception of Dan and Venus who were traveling as stowaways in her straw purse, were being shipped. "A-Dios!" Miss Rose called again as she was walking away.

Stormy swallowed hard and pulled out a Kleenex from her pocket. "Miss Rose, can't you give me a hug before you go?" she called.

Miss Rose turned back. She gave them each a hug and a kiss on the cheek. Then she said, "Carmen, girl, Miss Rose is never going to forget you. Whenever you need anything, *anything*, you remember Miss Rose. Miss Rose will always keep a special candle burning just for you, baby!" Miss Rose patted the garnet rose brooch Carmen had bought for her to pin on her tignon—the "right" name for Miss Rose's turban, as she had told Carmen many times.

Carmen nodded. Miss Rose went off. "Man!" Stormy said as they got back into her limo, urged on by a policeman to keep the traffic moving, "I am sure gonna miss that loca, aren't you?"

◁ By Way of
Acknowledgments

You get a call from your agent and friend, Susan Bergholz, one day in winter, but you're in Florida so you can't really tell. Best news of the day. Gerald Howard, your editor at W. W. Norton, has come through for you again and sent the contract. Can you have the short stories in by August? Sure, of course. Oh, you mean *this* August? Hmm.

The National Endowment for the Arts despite attacks has advanced unbelievably good news. You have received *a second* fellowship—this one in fiction!

Many things happen around you between then and August, big things, feasts with friends in Berlin and elsewhere, no famine perhaps, but a murderous heat wave in Chicago where you find yourself in summer with no air conditioning, the agony of love and war: life's usual bill of fare.

But by then, you are once again Ana de Aire with no place to write . . . or paint . . . or think, scattered by the wind that surrounds your fate. Your comadre Juana Guzmán, your sister Bea Martínez, and your mamacita dearest (despite their own hardships) come to your aid, supplying pens and paper, and help set up La Doña's Emergency Headquarters in a basement; and every night, when its dankness is preferable to the suffocating house, you write and write.

And the women, mujeres bien apasionadas que te llaman, que te escriben, que no te dejan rajar—they hold you steady so that you *will* write, when pens, paper, and space aren't enough. One even threatens to come over in dominatrix leather to crack the whip. Another sends rain sticks and amaranth from Tepoztlan to keep your energy free-flowing. Yet another buys a fax machine for the sole purpose of your sending midnight drafts if you so desire. Susan B. is always there; and when Madame B. goes to Russia, she brings back vodka for your next visit in New York. Gerry is there with the quiet faith of those so far from God. George is there—in search of Miss Rose with you in New Orleans, and Juana Gallo in Zacatecas. You write your way through the heat wave, the hijo-at-large (who challenges you to operate at cyber-Amazon capacity when he doesn't return on schedule at summer's end), lawyers and court dates, the illnesses, death, more love pangs and another war: life's usual bill of fare.

One cloud-laden afternoon in August you announce, to no one in particular, to everyone at once, at first in a whisper, then with a shout: the stories are done. And the sky breaks in a thunderous storm. (It really does!) You thank everyone and everything, the spirits, the saints, and Our Mother who never leaves you; you thank the frijoles of the day and the glass of vino tinto you permit yourself in the evening after a good night's writing. You thank all the men and all the women who love you for the sake of the pen and for your sake and you love them, too.

A todos por todo y tanto, gracias. All I have to thank you

with are these stories. Although they are not much, I hope you enjoy them, perhaps find a little something here to lift your heart.

A.C.
April 1996
Chicago